The Extraordinary eTab
of Julian Newcomber

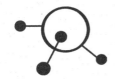

THE EXTRA-ORDINARY eTab of JULIAN NEWCOMBER

by michael seese

COMMON DEER PRESS

Published by Common Deer Press Incorporated.

Published in 2018 by Common Deer Press
3203-1 Scott St.
Toronto, ON
M5V 1A1

Library of Congress Cataloging-in-Publication Data
Seese, Michael.—First edition.
The Extraordinary eTab of Julian Newcomber/ Michael Seese
ISBN 978-1-988761-28-2 (print)
ISBN 978-1-988761-29-9 (e-book)

Cover Image: © Rekka Bell
Book Design: Ellie Sipila

Printed in Canada

WWW.COMMONDEERPRESS.COM

THIS BOOK IS DEDICATED TO THE UNIVERSE, WHICH HAS A STRANGE SENSE OF HUMOR, MAINLY BECAUSE I "INSIST ON POKING A FINGER IN ITS EYE."

CHAPTER 1

"Hey Pickle!"

The words thundered off the brick walls of Whispering Falls Intermediate School, loosening a few in the process. Time stood still, almost as if someone had begun a giant game of cosmic freeze tag. Balls stopped bouncing. Swings stopped swinging. Sneakers stopped squeaking. In fact, all recess activities and shenanigans came to a screeching halt while the fourth, fifth, and sixth graders scanned the skies on an otherwise fine October day, searching for the approaching storm. Julian didn't need to look. He knew that doom clung close to the ground because that nasal voice followed by a partial eclipse of the sun could mean only one thing.

Biff.

And Julian was *not* in the mood to deal with him. Not now. Not today. Not tomorrow. Truth be told, not in a duotrigintillion years or forever, whichever came first. But not today, especially, since Julian had other insurmountable problems to worry about.

Unfortunately, the human oak tree with size-nine

shoes and breath like microwaved bacon had a different agenda. Julian's hope for an uneventful start to the day came to a screeching halt as Biff Masterson, a good head-and-a-half taller, more if you factored in the mohawk, lumbered in front of him and planted his big feet.

"Pickle, I was talking to you, Pickle. Are you deaf or something, Pickle?"

Julian figured out early on that Biff seemed to like saying the word "pickle." Or any word associated with food, for that matter. He could not understand why someone *born* to be a bully—his real name was Spike after all—would choose to go by "Biff."

"Sorry, Biff. I didn't realize you were talking to me. You said 'pickle.' And I don't know anyone by that name. So I assumed you were thinking out loud about your lunch. Or your breakfast. Or your mid-morning snack. Now if you'll excuse me," he said, stepping around the forest of one. As the new kid in school (the label applied to him more often than he would have liked), Julian had become very good—what the smart folks call "adept"—at analyzing a situation and getting out of it. The skill had served him well on many occasions, in many situations. Each school, he'd found, offered its own unique brand of bully. At Fairpark Elementary, a good day was any day he managed to avoid Mace Winshaft (apparently, his parents *really* loved *Star Wars*), who would crack walnuts by placing them against his own forehead and hitting them with a hammer, or a brick, or a Buick, or whatever might have been handy. At Brady Lower Upper

Middle School, his tormentor—what the smart folks call "nemesis"—was Maurice Evans, who owned a pet orangutan that he slept with, and wrestled with, and fought for table scraps with. (On Halloween he would send Zaius to school in his place, and no one could tell the difference.) Before that, it was Bertha Patton, who was in a league all her own.

"Your name is Newcomber," Biff snorted, coming around like the USS *Missouri* and blocking the path yet again. Like a plant-eating dinosaur, he was slow of foot, with a brain to match. But he covered so much ground and filled so much space that getting around him required a trip, bordering on an excursion. "That sounds like cucumber. And cucumbers are just like pickles. So, you're Pickle."

Biff's mouth watered a little as he said it, which disturbed Julian even more.

"No, pickles are *made from* cucumbers," Julian said. "But not all cucumbers become pickles. Using your thinking, pencils are just like trees."

"No, they're not. You can't write with a tree."

"You know, you are absolutely right. They're not. Hey, hold that thought for a minute. Or a second, if sixty of them is too much for you."

Julian figured the complex math would tax Biff's brain long enough to buy him the time he needed to end this stupid—what the smart folks call "inane"—conversation ASAP. He knew that what he was about to do would be less than wise. *Potentially catastrophic, though probably not cataclysmic,* Julian thought, using two words from this week's spelling lesson. But someone he read about in a history book had said something like "Desperate times call for desperate measures." He reached into his backpack, pulled out the Extraordinary eTab, unrolled it, swiped the screen, and tapped the pulsating icon with the over-crowded clock. He heard *the* sound and saw *the* light. A moment later, Julian found himself sitting at his desk in the comfort of his classroom. Fortunately, his techno-magical appearance went unnoticed in the bustle and jostle of the mad dash to the desks in the precious seconds before the bell. He breathed a sigh of relief as he waited for Mrs. Stern to call his name.

"Spike Masterson? Spike? Tardy. Again," she clucked, making a little tick mark on her attendance sheet.

Julian hadn't expected that to happen. But when it came to the eTab—or any of his dad's inventions— Julian had learned to expect the unexpected. Not to mention the unlikely, the bizarre, the absurd, the im-probable, and/or the downright impossible.

"Julian Newcomber?"

"Here, Mrs. Stern."

"Good."

She continued on down the list and completed the roll call.

"Now, class, please open your math books and memorize pages fifty to the end." Julian flipped to page four hundred ninety-six. "There will be a test on this material tomorrow."

Silence clung to the classroom as twenty-four anx-ious souls waited to hear the magical words: "Just kidding." When they failed to materialize, the children's groans rivaled those of the old school's heating system.

Julian obediently opened his book and pretended to read, just like Mrs. Stern did when she sat at her desk and "read" her teacher's study guide, even though she was actually sleeping with her eyes open (the snoring always gave it away). But instead of studying his multiplication tables, Julian began planning. He just needed to get through the school day and get home. Today he had a bigger problem to deal with.

He had to figure how to help himself—specifically, his twenty-year-old self—go back in time to undo a mistake that could pollute the natural timeline, rewrite history, and change the world as we know it.

No pressure.

CHAPTER 2

Perhaps a little history—what the smart folks call "background" and the literary smart folks call "exposition"—would be in order.

Julian Newcomber, twelve years of age and wise beyond those twelve years, was the oldest son of Abigail and Andrew Newcomber. His mom, according to Grandma and Grandpa Newcomber, was a born homemaker. To some people, the word "homemaker" would be another way of saying "stay-at-home mom." But in the case of Mrs. Newcomber, it meant more than that. A lot more. Julian's dad was an inventor. And a lot of his inventions didn't work quite the way he planned. To be more accurate, they failed. Badly. Really badly. So badly, in fact, they often wrecked the Newcomber house. Hence the need for Mrs. Newcomber to be a homemaker, in the literal sense of the word.

To say Mr. Newcomber's inventions *always* failed would be a lie.

One invention that did work really well was the Expand-O-House. The Expand-O-House was a plain—what the smart folks call "nondescript"—box, about a foot on each side. Julian wasn't sure exactly what was inside of it or what made it work. All he knew was that his dad would put one on the ground in the middle of a big empty lot, push a few buttons and then run backward as fast as he could. Within seconds, lights would start lighting, flaps would start flapping, and walls would start...walling. Two minutes later, there would be a brand-new house sitting there, complete with a basketball pole in the driveway, two cars in the garage, and a white picket fence surrounding it all.

Mrs. Newcomber, always the planner, made sure to keep a ready supply of Expand-O-Houses stashed away in a safe, and boom-proof, place. So whenever one house went skyward, all she has to do was retrieve one and let her husband do his thing. Then she would do her homemaker thing. Julian wasn't exactly sure *how* she did it. That is, how she managed to fill the new house with new furniture, dishes, clothes, food, and the hamsters, as all of those things cost money. He assumed it had something to do with her other job, which she called "day trading."

Julian had once asked his dad what day trading was. He'd answered, "Anyone can spot a leopard, but your mother is the only person I know who can spot a leopard without its spots." Mr. Newcomber often didn't make sense, especially on the days a lot of brightly colored smoke spewed from his workshop. Leopards aside, Mrs. Newcomber must have been good at it, as many days Julian witnessed the following exchange between his parents.

Mr. Newcomber: "How did we do today?"

Mrs. Newcomber: "Up three thousand."

Mr. Newcomber: "Happy Dance time!"

And though he could have put the new house where the old one had been, Mr. Newcomber thought someone—the news or the neighbors or the police—might ask a lot of questions along the lines of, "Why are there pieces of a house lying all over the place?" So, the family would usually just move, far away, find a vacant lot in a new city, and start over again.

Which is why Julian was always the new kid in school.

And as if his parents' foibles and follies weren't burden enough, Julian also had to contend with two siblings, twins Dylan and Olivia. Mostly, he thought they were nothing more than dorky little kids who hounded him constantly. After all, they were *three* years younger. Though, as Dylan liked to remind Julian, it actually was two years and eight months. And soon, there would no longer be a three-year difference, since their birthday was coming up. Regardless of the numerical technicalities, Julian felt older. Still, sometimes he wondered whether something more was going on with them, as funny stuff seemed to follow them around, like a dog you'd shared your sandwich with. He'd have to look into that someday.

The point is that Mr. Newcomber's inventions either:

Exploded.

Worked.

Or sort of worked. Which is to say they *did* work, only not in the way Mr. Newcomber had planned.

Which brings us to the Extraordinary eTab...

CHAPTER 3

The intercom that Julian's father had installed in Julian's room buzzed, though "shrieked like a cat whose tail had gotten stepped on repeatedly" would be a more apt description. It was his dad, trying to get his attention.

Mission accomplished.

"Julian, could you please come out to the workshop? I want to show you something."

Julian put on his football helmet and the Kevlar fireplace gloves, then went out the back door.

"Yes, Dad?" he said, sticking a cautious head into the barn, now his dad's workshop, in the back yard. *Way* in the back yard. *Way* at the back of their property, and safely away from their house. *Though dangerously close to the high-voltage electrical wires overhead*, Julian often thought.

"Check out—what the more casual folks call 'take a gander at'—this," Mr. Newcomber said, holding up a black piece of paper.

"What is it?"

"What does it look like?"

"A piece of blank black paper."

"You've got it, son. Ta-da! I've invented blank black paper!"

"You have an answer for everything, don't you Dad?"

"I like to think so. Sometimes, it's even the right answer."

Mrs. Newcomber often said her husband's sense of humor was somewhat of an acquired taste. Fortunately (or not), Julian had been fed a steady diet of it for twelve years, and by now, was pretty much immune to it.

"No, really, Dad. What is it?"

"Take it," Mr. Newcomber said, rolling it into a tube and floating it over to his son, despite the fact that it looked like it had no business flying, let alone alighting perfectly in Julian's receptive palms.

Weighing it in his hands, it seemed heavier than an ordinary piece of paper. Much heavier.

Julian unrolled it and examined it closely. He couldn't see how the thin (though heavy) paper could be anything else.

"What does it do?" he asked.

"Turn it on," Mr. Newcomber said.

"Turn it on? How?"

"Run a finger across it."

Julian still had on the football helmet. But he wished he had been wearing his swim goggles as well, just to be safe. He took off one glove, closed one eye, and swept a finger across the page. A previously unseen screen lit up, and a small army of icons marched out of the corners and circled the surface before taking their places in neat—what the smart folks call "precise" or "orderly"—rows and columns.

"What do you think?"

"I've never seen a piece of blank black paper do that before."

"That's because it's really not a piece of blank black paper."

"And I'll just bet you've given it a name."

"I will not accept such a wager, because I would lose. I call it the eTab."

"The eTab?"

"Yes!" Mr. Newcomber proclaimed as he assumed a heroic superhero, hands-on-his-hips pose and stuck his chin in the air. "Ready for this? It stands for Experimental Talking Analog...Bagpipe."

"Bagpipe?"

"I'm still working on the last word."

"Oh. I thought it stood for Electronic Tablet."

"Oooh! That's good, too. I need to remember that. Let me get a pen."

As Mr. Newcomber scribbled, Julian looked at the eTab from every angle, in order. Acute. Right. Obtuse.

"Cool! What apps does it have?"

"Everything."

"Really, Dad? Everything?"

"OK, not *everything*. There's no refrigerator. But email, the internet, a word processor, a camera, the weather, not the weather itself, but the weather report. Not to mention four hundred fifty-three thousand songs, television stations from eighteen countries—I'm working on the rights for some others—as well as every textbook you will need through high school and, depending on where you go to college—"

"Great," Julian said, less than excited about the latter. "I'm sure this will help a lot with—Wait! Did you say *talking?*"

"I think I did!" said Mr. Newcomber, clearly excited about that feature. "Ask it something. Anything."

"OK. What is the temperature today in Antarctica?"

"Was sagen Sie? Ich verstehe nicht."

"What?" asked Julian.

"Hmmm," said Mr. Newcomber. "I did get a lot of the parts from this mail order place in Berlin. Maybe you should just forget about talking to it for now. Or, study German."

"What does this do?" Julian asked, pointing to the *large,* brightly glowing clock icon in the lower right-hand corner. A clock with a lot of numbers. Julian stopped counting at fifty. He could have counted higher. He just didn't want to.

"That? It's a clock."

Julian said nothing. He'd come to understand that his dad had a habit of pausing for dramatic effect.

"And it's something you're going to *love!* I call it the Dad Five-Minute Warning app. Did I mention you'll love it? You know how you're always asking me for something, and I'm always saying, 'Give me five more minutes,' which more often than not manages to stretch out to five days?" Mr. Newcomber asked, too excited to wait for an answer, or breathe. "Well, if you tap that icon, my cell phone will ring, and the eTab will start a five-minute timer. After five minutes, my phone will ring again. If, after one more minute, I haven't tapped the icon on your eTab myself—it recognizes my fingerprint—then my cell phone will shock me with one hundred milliamps. Don't worry. It's not enough to kill me or anything. It will just get my attention. Wait...or should that be volts? I never could keep those two potentially lethal units of measurement straight. I'd better test it on something. Something living. But not living like a plant. Living and breathing. Well, plants do breathe, but—"

"How about Dylan?"

"Yes, Dylan breathes as well."

"No. I mean, how about testing it on Dylan?"

Julian, like all big brothers, enjoyed torturing his younger brother whenever possible. If he could trick his dad into testing the jolt on Dylan, that would be a major score—what the smart folks call a "coup" (with a silent *p*).

"Yeah, no," Mr. Newcomber said, scratching his head with enough distracted energy to send a tempest of ripples through his hair, which people often mistook for a mop or topiary. "Hmmm, a squirrel. I wonder if I can catch a squirrel. How does one catch a squirrel? Oh, I know, I can—"

"Does it work anywhere?" Julian asked, his voice rising with excitement.

"What?" Mr. Newcomber said, lifting up the welding mask he already had put on—what the smart folks call "donned"—and turning off the blowtorch he already had lit—what the smart folks call "ignited."

"That shocking thing. Will it work anywhere?"

"As in, anywhere on the planet? I think so. Off the planet? That would require some testing. Not to mention a propulsion system that rocks. But it sure would be a fun challenge—"

"Earth to Dad. So, anywhere?"

"What? Yes, anywhere."

"YES! You are so—"

"But its range is limited. You have to be within about one hundred feet of me. Silly Man! Your dad's not stupid, you know."

"I know. One hundred feet, huh? So, what happens if I run the app when I'm farther away?"

"Nothing, I suppose. Or who knows? Maybe it'll send you to another place. Another time. Another dimension," he said, waving his fingers like a mystic. "A place, a time, a dimension where little boys pick up their rooms and eat their broccoli."

"That place doesn't exist, Dad."

"Probably not. But I can hope. Or, I can invent it..."

Julian would have laughed. But when his dad did that staring-off-into-the-distance thing, Julian knew he was performing mathematical computations, drawing diagrams in his head, and planning a trip to Home Depot.

"Thanks, Dad. I mean it. I do. This is really great. I'm going to go try it out. Can I test the—"

"Of course. And you can bet your bippy I'll be there within five minutes. Just don't run and hide.

That's dishonest *and* evil—what the smart folks call 'conniving.' And be sure to try out the other features as well. Now, where was I?" Mr. Newcomber said, his mind already disengaged from the conversation with Julian. "Oh yeah, catching a squirrel. I'll need some sort of bait. And an electro-magnetic generator to stun him. Or her. Just a little. I imagine a fried squirrel would smell to high..."

Julian took the eTab and went back to the house, assuming it would be at least five minutes before his dad noticed he'd left. He decided not to test the clock right away. He knew his dad would be busily focused on his *obsession du jour*, building a better squirrel trap. What he didn't know, but soon would learn, was that his dad had a weird talent—what the smart folks call an "uncanny knack"—for saying something as a joke but having it come true.

CHAPTER 4

Julian spent several weeks testing out the various apps his dad had installed on the eTab. Among his favorites were Sounds And Smells Of The Amazon Rain Forest, Virtual Volcano Diver, and US Navy Submarine Cam. Julian suspected that last one might get his dad in real hot water, or whatever happens to misbehaving sailors these days, if the Navy ever found out about it.

But the coolest, he decided, was one called Bother Bill. It allowed Julian to take command of the TV dish on the roof of the house across the street, and point it at...well, anywhere *but* the satellite circling high above the Earth in a fixed—what the smart folks call "stationary" and the *really* smart scientific folks call "geosynchronous"—orbit. Julian suspected his dad meant to keep that one for himself, seeing as how Mr. Newcomber always complained about Bill's dog doing its business in their front yard. (If the windows happened to be open when Mr. Newcomber discovered one of Napoleon's "gifts," Julian would learn a few new choice words.)

Otherwise, most of the apps worked pretty much as expected. The email app did indeed send and receive emails. The internet browser did indeed browse the internet. And the word processor did indeed process words.

Indeed, everything worked normally which, when speaking of his dad's inventions, was highly *abnormal*. But then one day, something extraordinary happened...

While walking home, Julian decided to conduct a little experiment. About seven-eighths or perhaps eight-ninths of the way there—the point being, more than one hundred feet away from the house—he pulled out the eTab, unrolled it, and swiped.

"I wonder if I'm close enough?" he said. A mischievous grin came to his face. He tapped the large clock icon, expecting one of two things to happen.

Nothing.

Or, he would casually walk through the door in a few minutes and find his dad frantically looking for him.

(Actually, a third option crossed his mind just as finger met eTab. Fortunately, the house did not go *KABOOM!*)

But what *did* happen was the last thing he would have expected. There was a sound, kind of like the sound the vacuum cleaner makes. (Of course, since his dad had built theirs, it didn't sound like a *normal* vacuum cleaner.) Then came a flash of light. Not painfully bright, but bright enough to make him blink. It was mostly like a camera flash, but without the little pre-flash flash. The next thing he knew, he was not walking home, but *at* home, sitting at the kitchen table, with his mother across the room fixing his snack.

"Mom?" Julian said, feeling a little off.

His mom whirled around, eyes wide, hand on her heart.

"Boy! You sure came out of nowhere."

"Mom. I feel kind of—"

"Hungry?"

Julian was about to say, "stretched like a rubber band, flung across the room, and slammed unceremoniously into a brick wall." But he thought his mother might take that as a sign of an impending illness of some sort and sprint him to the doctor.

"That too."

"I'll bet. Your snack's almost ready, Little Man."

The kitchen clock read 4:03.

Julian started to think. Quickly.

Normally, walking at a brisk pace would get him home a bit before four. Two minutes, maybe three. That meant he had probably tapped the clock icon at 3:57. And it was now 4:03, meaning...

Somehow, he had traveled *six minutes into the future!*

I need to tell Dad about this, he thought. *Right away! Right now!*

At that moment, his mother put a bowl of chicken noodle soup *and* a s'more in front of him.

It can wait.

After finishing his snack, Julian went out to the workshop.

"Dad?" he said, walking in.

"Julian. You're not wearing a helmet," Mr. Newcomber said as he put down some sort of electrical-looking thing. The squirrel desperately pacing in the cage on the table breathed a sigh of relief.

"Yeah, I must be feeling brave—what the smart folks call 'courageous'—today. Can I ask you something? That app. The clock. How does it work?"

"It works like a clock. No, that's not accurate. It works like an egg timer. You hit the button, it buzzes my cell phone, and I have five minutes—plus a one-minute grace period—to touch your eTab. Didn't we talk about this?"

"Yeah, we did. But my question is, how does it *work?*"

"An interesting question. To be completely honest, I'm not sure. I downloaded the code from some website I found. And then I made a few changes—what the smart folks call 'modifications,' or sometimes 'enhancements.' And among software developers, 'scope creep.' That sure is a lot of smart folks' words."

"It is. Anyway, what kinds of changes?"

"Nothing major. The biggest one I had to come up with was figuring out some way to have it ring my cell phone, and then wait five plus one minutes. I thought about that one for a long time."

"And by 'long time' you mean..."

"Seven minutes. Maybe eight. And then I hit upon an igneous solu—make that *ingenious*—solution.

Though, considering what my creations often do, 'igneous' isn't a bad alternative."

At least he realizes it, Julian thought.

"Finally, what I decided made the most sense would be to set up a logical feedback loop, so everything else could keep running without the clock app interfering."

"Would that thing you mentioned—the logical feedback loop—do anything else?"

"It shouldn't. Why do you ask?"

"I don't know. A feedback loop sounds like something from a science fiction movie. You know, warping space and time.

"Well, then, let me think. Though I much prefer the sound of 'ruminate,' which I not to be confused with what cows, smart or otherwise, do when they—"

"Dad."

"OK, thinking now."

Julian could tell by the look on his dad's face that he really was thinking carefully about the question.

"No," Mr. Newcomber finally said.

"No? Are you sure?"

"Yes."

"You're sure there is no way it could—" Julian stopped himself before saying "somehow either compress time and/or launch me six minutes into the future."

"Could what?"

"Nothing. Never mind. Thanks, Dad."

Julian knew his dad was smart. Very smart. But he

also knew something really out of the ordinary had happened on his walk home today.

He went back into the house and told his mom he would be in his room, doing his homework, studying for a big test. He ran upstairs, closed and locked the door, sat down on his bed, and looked at the eTab.

Over the course of the past few weeks he had tried every other app on the eTab, and they all seemed to work normally. (That statement was not one hundred percent true; there was one app called ePie In The Face that just begged to be left alone.)

Julian weighed his options. Whenever his dad faced a challenge, he would roll up his sleeves and dive right in, which is why the hair on his forearms and his eyebrows was often singed. His mother, on the other hand, tended to approach things more cautiously, though the phrase she preferred was "with a least a minimum sense of sanity, Andrew."

Julian teeter-tottered between the two, waving his finger, back and forth and back and forth, and around and around and around, over the icon. He wanted to—and at the same time didn't want to—touch it.

He made up his mind.

Julian, like his dad, enjoyed experimenting—what his mom called "risking life and limb and house on some cockamamie whim." But in order to experiment, one needs a plan. Julian grabbed a pen, a pad of paper, and a thinking cap. He pondered a moment, then wrote:

STEP 1: TRY IT AGAIN.

(As he grew older and improved his would-be mad scientist skills, Julian would learn to add to—what the smart folks call "flesh out"—his plans.)

Recalling that his previous temporal travel had left him feeling woozy, weird, and generally out of whack, he sat down at his desk so he wouldn't have as far to fall.

He swiveled the alarm clock on his nightstand so he could see the face, a strange term, he always thought, since digital clocks don't have faces like those old-fashioned ones his parents preferred. Of course, one of the reasons they preferred them was that his sister Olivia expressed her "artistic angst," to use his mom's words (which Julian vaguely understood, but not really), by painting funny faces on them.

4:59.

One minute until 5:00.

Julian decided it was karma, or kismet, or one of those other terms meaning the same thing as fate, that he now stood (or sat, actually) on the verge of a new hour.

He waited, his finger at the ready, for the demise of the 4:00 hour and the ascension of its successor, managing to work three vocabulary words into a single thought. He closed his eyes, waited through a moment of eternity, then opened them.

4:59.

Close. Wait. Open.

4:59.

Repeat.

4:59.

4:59.

Julian wished he had an old-fashioned clock, since most of those antique timepieces had second hands on them.

4:59.

4:59.

4:59.

5:00.

5:00.

5:00.

Oops.

Lulled into lethargy by the clock's stubborn refusal to let go of the previous hour, he lost a few precious seconds that otherwise could have been devoted to his experiment/cockamamie whim.

"OK, this is it," he said.

Julian stationed his finger directly over the icon of mystery, closed his eyes, and tapped. The vacuum cleaner sound filled the room, and the flash imprinted itself on his retina even behind closed eyelids.

Silence settled around him.

"When I open my eyes," he said to reassure himself, "it will be either 5:00 or 5:06." Though in the back of his mind a little voice said, *Or next year. You know your dad.* He breathed out and prepared to learn once and for all whether the weird episode this afternoon was an accident or a permanent and scary-fascinating feature of the eTab

"OK. I'm going to open my eyes now. Yup. Going to open them. Opening them in three…two…"

KnockKnockKnockKnockKnockKnock.

Julian wheeled around.

"Yes?"

"Julian?" came his dad's not exactly panicked, though clearly urgent, voice.

"Yes, Dad?"

"Can I come in?"

"I'm doing homework."

"I'm glad to hear it. That kind of dedicated—what the smart folks call 'industrious'—attitude will take you far in life. But may I interrupt you a minute? I'd like to come in before my cell phone zaps me. I haven't, as of yet, finished my squirrel testing."

It dawned on Julian that in his eagerness to earn his Boy Scout time altering merit badge, he had lost sight of the true purpose of the Dad Five-Minute Warning app. To call his dad and give him a *really* good reason—what the smart folks call "incentive"— to come running.

"Yeah, Dad. Sure," he said, hustling over and unlocking the door.

Mr. Newcomber zipped in, quickly scanned the room for the instrument of his discomfort (a far cry from an "instrument of destruction," but still...) then headed straight toward the eTab.

"Whew!" he said, deactivating the jolt-to-be.

"Sorry about that, Dad."

"No worries. So, what do you want?"

"Want?"

"You're supposed to use the app to get me when you need something. To prevent me from saying

'Give me five more minutes,' like I often do, and then taking a day or two to get back to—Didn't we talk about this as well?"

"We did."

"So?"

"So?"

"So, what do you need, Son?"

"Oh. Nothing. Sorry. False alarm. I must have hit it accidentally. My bad. I'll try to be more careful."

"Oh. No worries. OK. Whew. Well, see you at dinner."

Julian's dad shuffled out of the room, in all likelihood happy to know the Dad Five-Minute Warning app worked, and at the same time, happier to know he didn't have to find out exactly how well.

Julian grabbed the pen again.

STEP 2: TRY IT AGAIN, SOMEWHERE AT LEAST 100 FEET FROM THE HOUSE.

At precisely 5:20, Julian sat strategically in a carrel in a corner of the Whispering Falls Public Library. Since it was just before dinnertime in Whispering Falls (as well as most of the eastern standard time zone) the place was largely deserted. And quiet. At least it would be, until he implemented Step 2 and unleashed the vacuum cleaner/jet engine sound on the unsuspecting patrons, staff, and neighbors, that is.

The face of the big round library clock stared back at him. The temperamental tablet lay on the table before him. Julian wanted to wait, but he couldn't. He needed to be done by 5:55 so he could hurry home in time for his dinner. And given the uncertainty of the whole time-shifting enterprise, a technical oopsie— what the smart folks call a "glitch"—could whisk him any number of minutes or weeks beyond 5:55. And if that happened, he would be late and his mom almost certainly would launch her Shriek Like A Banshee app, which wasn't really an app, but somehow just part of her "operating system," and which was loud enough to be heard over the fire truck sirens at the Whispering Falls Memorial Day parade.

Julian fixed his focus on the thin black metal strip of the clock's second hand as it began the painfully slow journey through the latter half of the minute. When it pointed straight up, Julian didn't hesitate. He tapped the clock app. As he expected, loud sound, bright flash. Luckily, no librarian came rushing over to *ssshhhh* him for it. When the 4th of July celebration in his eyes concluded (he made a mental note to add another step: wear sunglasses) the library clock confirmed his suspicions.

5:26.

So now what do I do? he wondered.

In theory, he could have repeated the experiment to see if the world would fast-forward from 5:26 to 5:32, which seemed to be the most logical outcome. But Julian decided the exercise was somewhat pointless. What if the next time jump moved life ahead five minutes? Or seven minutes? What would be the significance? None, really. Moving through time was moving through time. Unless...

Julian drummed his fingers on the worn laminate tabletop. What if there were some way to intentionally alter the time jump? To *make* it longer? He drummed his fingers some more.

He studied the clock app icon. The hands appeared to be fixed, mere multicolored pixels, just like the rest of the icon. He checked the app's settings. But other than a "Help" button which, when pressed played a recorded message from his dad saying, "Time? Time to brush your teeth! Gotcha!" there was nothing.

Then came a flash of inspiration.

Both the library clock and the eTab clock showed 5:29. Julian opened the settings again, set the device's time ahead ten minutes, and exited out to the main screen. The eTab now showed 5:40. The wall clock read 5:30. Without hesitation he tapped and waited through the customary fireworks—what the smart folks call "pyrotechnics." Once things quieted down, he peeked with one wary eye. The wall clock now showed 5:46! Six minutes ahead of the time he told his eTab it was, and sixteen minutes ahead of the time it had truly been when he started

That, he classified as noteworthy.

It would also prove life-altering, though Julian could not know it at the time.

STEP 3: GO BACK IN TIME.

His next temporal excursion, Julian decided, should be to go back in time. But to when...

He drummed his fingers a final time.

I enjoyed today's after-school snack. I could go back to the walk home.

Ooh! Or I messed up last week's history test. I could zip back, retake it, and be home before dinner.

Or...

He paused. Just the other day he'd sat down on the couch with his dad, who happened to be watching a classic old movie called *Back to the Future* about a high school kid who drives a car so fast he goes back in time. He lands on the day his parents met, interferes with them meeting, and has to spend the rest of the movie trying to undo his oopsie. So, having witnessed firsthand Marty McSomebody's potentially life-or-not-ever-alive race against time to unite his parents and invent rock and roll, Julian vowed to never use the eTab to go back in time. After all, who could know what chaos might be unleashed?

An on-and-off buzzing sound caught his attention. It went *buzz*...pause...*buzz*...pause.

A big green telephone icon flashed in sync with the buzz. It went glow...off...glow...off. He touched it, cautiously, as always.

His dad's face popped onto the screen.

"Dad?"

"Hi, Julian. Your mother has let me know *quite clearly* that dinner is in thirteen minutes. I thought I'd warn you before she starts wondering where you might be hiding and decides to unleash the Scream Of Infinity, as I like to call it."

"That's funny, Dad. That name. Hey, I didn't know we could talk over this thing."

"We couldn't. At least not until now, after my last software push. As part of it, you also have…."

"Software push?"

"Yeah. I occasionally need to send a software update to the eTab. It all happens in the background. Anyway, I was looking at family cell phone plans this afternoon. I figured it was about time for you to have a phone. And boy! Do you have any idea how expensive those calling and texting and data and whatever else plans are? I think my first car payment was less. So, I thought I'd figure out a way to leverage Wi-Fi and piggyback on the encrypted data stream over the 802.11x protocol and—I'm confusing you, aren't I?"

"You always do, Dad."

"Consistency has always been an important part— what the smart folks call 'a mainstay'—of my game. Unfortunately, the range is limited. Five hundred feet. Three miles, tops. Though if I could get my hands on the source code the phone companies use…"

"I'm at the library. I'll be home in five minutes. Tell Mom. And thanks for the heads-up, Dad."

Julian pressed the telephone icon again, rolled up the eTab, and raced home, arriving just as his mom was completing her deep-breathing exercises in preparation for the Banshee Blast Of Infinity, his new name for the tsunami of sound.

"Oh, good. You're here," she said sweetly before exhaling for a good thirty seconds.

At the dinner table, Julian's fork attacked his food while his mind attacked the good and bad points of limited time travel.

(Actually, he could devote only a portion of his brain to considering several reasonably harmless applications of time travel because he needed to stay engaged enough to take part in the required family dinnertime discussion.)

What could I do if I jumped ahead ten, twenty, or thirty minutes? he thought.

He could excuse himself from the table for a minute, run one hundred and one feet down the street, and skip ahead to dessert, bypassing dinner and, more to the point, the broccoli.

He could jump to the end of the baseball game on TV, then go back and make a bet with his dad as to who would win. However, he realized that doing so would violate his stated vow to never jump back in time, which also ruled out skipping ahead thirty minutes to the post-exam answer review in class, then going back to take the test.

But his thoughts—what the dreamy folks call "flights of fancy"—remained rooted in the innocent fascination of a twelve-year-old brain, and he never considered possibilities beyond his limited world.

In time—years, to be imprecise—he would.

CHAPTER 5

"Wake up, Little Sleepy Man. Let me see that adorable bedhead of yours."

"Aw, Mom. It's too early. Just six more minutes."

"*Six* minutes? Why the crooked number, slugger?" Mrs. Newcomber asked. Contrary to stereotypes, it was Mrs. Newcomber who was the baseball fan of the family. (Mr. Newcomber, on the other hand, preferred Australian rules football, which as far as Julian could tell, had no actual rules.) As such she would sprinkle, if not ladle, terms like "crooked numbers," "can of corn," and "put some mustard on it" into conversations. Her love of the great American pastime came as no surprise to Julian. Mr. Newcomber often pointed out that his wife, in her pre-wife days, had been a pretty awesome—what the smart folks call "formidable"—fast-pitch softball player. Ever modest, Mrs. Newcomber would dismiss his comment with an "aw, shucks" wave of her hand. But at dinner, if Julian asked her to pass him a roll, she would put enough "pepper" on it to leave a red mark emblazoned on the center of his chest if he failed to snag the whole wheat fireball.

"You've got five," she said, displaying the sense of humor that at times seemed indistinguishable from her husband's. "If you're not down there in, now it's four-and-a-half, *you're outta here*."

With a dramatic sigh, Julian literally fell out of the top bunk, allowing him to take full advantage of the Tramp-O-Floor to spring across the room and into the clothes hanging in the InstaDressed Harness (two more of Mr. Newcomber's inventions, if you're keeping score) strung across the open closet door. Though both were exceptionally handy, suffice to say if Julian forgot to open his closet door before going to bed, their use made for a less-than-stellar start to the day.

Three-and-two-thirds-minutes later, Julian sat down to his sausage and cereal (not in the same bowl; that only happened when his dad fixed breakfast) and ate quietly. Of course, Dylan managed to fill the silence, as he always did.

"Mama? Mama? Mama? Mama? Mama? I don't think I can go to my piano lesson today, after school," he said.

"Why not?"

"I have a little headache."

"I'm sure it will be all better by the time you get home."

"But what if it's not Mama?"

"Trust me, sweetie. It will be."

"OK. But Mama? Mama? What if it's not?"

"Then Mama will take care of it," she said, pulling

from one of the drawers a power drill (kept there for that very purpose) and revving it up, all the while suppressing her evil smile.

"My head feels a lot better all of a sudden. And I'm hungry," Dylan said as he began shoveling cereal.

And serenity once again descended on the kitchen table.

After putting the twins on the bus (the elementary school did not lie within the comfy confines of the town, but rather out on the fringes of the county, about five minutes by car and an eternity by school bus), Mrs. Newcomber kissed Julian on the head and prepared to send him, independent boy that he was, on his way.

"Mom?" Julian asked. "Would you walk me to school?"

"Sure, Little Man."

They walked in silence while Julian's mouth tried to form the words his head wanted to say. He hadn't quite gotten there when his mom forced his hand. Or, mouth, as it were.

"So, what's up, Julian?"

At grown-up school, they must teach parents how to read their children's minds, Julian thought.

"Mom. If you could jump ahead, would you?"

"Do you mean like this?" she asked, planting a foot firmly and heaving herself a good eight feet down the sidewalk (Mrs. Newcomber also was long jumper in college). "Not too bad," she said, looking back at her launch point. "Though in all fairness, the slope here probably bought me another six inches."

"Truly impressive. But I don't mean jump ahead like that. I meant, in time."

"You're starting to sound like your father. Which may or may not be a good thing."

Julian assumed that was the sense of humor talking. He pressed on, "Well, would you?"

"Why would I want to?"

"I don't know. Maybe you have a hard day coming up. Maybe you have things you're not looking forward to. And you want to get them over with. Get them behind you. So, you jump ahead." A little something in a quiet corner of his brain whispered, *Are you sure you're not talking about yourself, and about almost any day, and about almost anywhere you've lived so far?* Julian shushed the voice, not wanting to think about the challenge of trying to fit in yet again, not to mention the looming jump up to a new school for grade seven.

"I know it's been tough on you. All this moving. But you should try to make some friends. Really try. Something tells me we're going to be here a while. I really think we've found our home."

"Good to know. But that's not what I was thinking." *Yup. Mindreading 101 at grown-up school.* "Well, maybe it was. A little. But my point is...No one really needs a car. You can walk everywhere. Especially here. In our *home*town." Julian liked the sound of that. "But we have cars, and we use things like cars, to make it easier on ourselves. What's different about skipping a day to make things easier on yourself?"

"You know, giving birth to you was quite an effort."

"It was?"

"They don't call it 'labor' for nothing, kiddo. Trust me, it was hard. What about that day? Should I have skipped that one?"

"Probably not."

"And even if jumping ahead meant I'd keep you, but just skip the pain...I'm still not sure I would."

"Why not?"

"Pain is a part of life. If you never know what pain feels like, then you probably won't know what real happiness feels like."

"Oh," was all he could think to say in the face of his mom's deep—what the smart folks call "profound"—8:00 a.m. philosophy lesson. Though it wasn't really what he wanted to know, it was something he *needed* to know.

"The point, Julian, is, every day—every moment of every day—is a gift. And if you keep refusing gifts..."

"Thanks, Mom," he said before hugging her, extra hard, and dashing up the concrete path.

On those occasions when Mr. Newcomber was feeling philosophical, he would say, "The universe has a strange sense of humor." Mrs. Newcomber usually would counter with something along the lines of "The universe enjoys whacking you upside the head because *you* insist on poking a finger in its eye."

Whatever the universe's motivation, on this day it must have been feeling particularly puckish—a term

Julian would not come to learn until eleventh grade, but from then on, would use in conversation whenever he could—as strange, inescapable references to *time* kept finding their way into his day.

The morning announcements concluded with a reminder to set clocks ahead the coming weekend because the *time would change.*

In English, the class read the poems "To Think of *Time*" by Walt Whitman, "Against that *time*, if ever that *time* come," by William Shakespeare, and "*Time* Long Past" by Percy Bysshe Shelley.

In science class, the teacher explained that in a vacuum, two objects will fall to Earth in the same amount of *time*, regardless of weight.

Even the cafeteria conspired to taunt him, as lunch was meatloaf and *twice-baked* potatoes which, in theory, could come from the kitchen of a time-traveling cook.

Given all the time signs circling his head like impatient vultures, Julian decided on the way home that he *had* to talk to his dad. After his snack.

Once the plates were in the sink and soaking, he went out back to the workshop. Mr. Newcomber was nowhere to be seen, meaning either he was not there, or he finally had succeeded in his quest to invent invisibility.

"Dad? DAD!"

No answer. Not there, it was.

Back in the house Julian found his mom, happily concocting something in the kitchen.

"Mom? Where's Dad?"

"He's at a conference with Dylan's teacher, Mrs. Malice."

"Don't you usually go to those sorts of things?"

His mom shrugged. Even though she didn't say it, Julian knew his mom was less than fond of Mrs. Malice. She probably sent Mr. Newcomber to the conference just to fluster, if not flummox, her.

Though Julian *really* wanted to speak with his dad, his absence offered an interesting, and potentially ill-fated, opportunity. With his dad out of the house, Julian could safely test some of the other theories he had concocted throughout the day, knowing his work would not be interrupted by a panicked paternal parent.

Upstairs, his after-school snack now a mere memory in his tummy, Julian and his co-conspirator the pen augmented The Plan.

STEP 4: CHANGE THE DATE.

The successfully tested hypothesis from last night's library experiment proved Julian could manually change the eTab clock, with the result being the six-minute jump would skip ahead based on the contrived time, as opposed to the actual time.

But what if he changed the calendar? Could he travel forward a day? Days? Weeks?

"How much worse could it be?" he asked, his less-than-mature brain not yet able to think through all the ramifications that would challenge, if not outright confound, even a more mature mind.

He thought long and hard about when he would want to travel ahead to.

Christmas morning, for obvious reasons.

His high school graduation, which would save him a lot of work.

Ultimately, he decided the safest choice would be trip to the near-future. Tomorrow. Tomorrow early, like 12:01 a.m. Worst case, Julian figured he would just be tired the next day, since he would miss a little sleep by discarding the two hours between 10:00 and 12:00. Though in light of the fact that yesterday he jumped to his seat at the kitchen table, he considered it a very real possibility he would find himself in bed, awake. Or perhaps asleep. In his pajamas. Or his clothes.

He began to superficially understand why time travel was confusing.

STEP 5: STOP WORRYING AND JUST DO IT!

Free from fear, seeing as how he was just following The Plan, Julian confidently tapped the gear icon on the eTab. The calendar loomed large, both on his screen and the little corner of his mind that wasn't totally on board with The Plan. He pushed the little blue box ahead, one space to the right. He OKed the change, then opened the clock and prepared to shave eight hours from his life.

"OK. All set," he said to no one. "I'm ready. Ready, willing, and able. OK, so I'm going to *do* it. It'll be fine. No problems at all. No *problema*." (He figured using a Spanish word could count as homework, in case his mom later asked what he had been doing.) Julian anguished for another minute.

"Really what could go wrong? Just a little tap. One little tap. One teeny tap. OK, so here I go. On three. One...two..."

He stopped when the vacuum cleaner noise filled the room.

"Wait! No! I didn't..." he said to the same no one. "Really, I..."

The sound came from the closet. The door was closed. But from around the edges shone a rectangular outline of light—what the smart folks call "a corona," though generally coronas are round. He got up, tiptoed over, and reached out, *now* feeling trepidation. He reached out, cautiously, toward the doorknob. His fingers inches away, the noise stopped, the light faded (or maybe it snapped off—Julian wasn't worried about the details), and the door flew open. Out stepped a grown-up. He stopped and looked every which way—up, down, left, right—amazed (though not as amazed as Julian). The man stood as still as a statue, taking in every detail of the room, except for the detail known as Julian, who by this time, had quietly faded into the wall, thankful that today he had worn his favorite shirt, the one colored eggshell matte. (Julian often wondered if there might be some connection between his mom's homemaking thing and the fact that everyone in the family had a lot of clothes matching the paint on the walls.) He thought about screaming. He wanted to scream. He prepared to scream. But for some reason he could not. He stared at the man, thinking something about him seemed somehow familiar.

"Who are—"

"Man! After ten years, you'd think I'd be used to that," the stranger said, stretching and twisting his neck, sending a sickening, yet impressive, cascade of crackles racing down his spine. "Wow! This room is just like I remember it."

"Just like you remember it? What do you mean?"

"This used to be my room," the man said.

"Are you the person who sold this house to my parents?" he asked.

"No, Silly Man. Don't you recognize me?"

Julian thought he might have. Sort of. But he didn't want to admit it.

"No," he lied.

"Julian, I'm you. Ten years from now. No, wait. Nine. No, wait again. Eight. Yes, eight. Seven? No, eight. Final answer."

"No you're not."

"Yes I am."

"You're lying!"

"I'm not."

"You don't look like you're from the future."

"What do you mean?"

"You're not wearing...I don't know, silver, shiny metal clothes. And you're not carrying a laser gun."

"I told you. I'm from ten years in the future. Scratch that. *Eight* years in the future. Not one hundred. We don't have those things. At least not yet. But as long as Dad is still inventing, who knows?"

"Fine. That makes sense. The silver clothing, laser gun part. But still, you can't be from the future."

"Yes I can."

"That's impossible. It can't be."

"It's not, and it can."

"But how—"

The stranger pulled from his pocket a slightly beat-up piece of blank black paper.

"Do you recognize this?" he asked.

"No," Julian said.

"Now *you're* lying. Of course you recognize it," the stranger said.

"OK. It's my eTab."

"Actually, it's *my* eTab. The eTab version 2.0, to be specific."

The man swiped. It came to life. All of the app icons were completely different. All except for one.

The Dad Five-Minute Warning app.

The familiar clock face was still there. It was huger, though. Way bigger than that of the eTab 1.0. And it had a lot of numbers. Way more than his.

"I made a few modifications," the man said.

"How do I know you're telling the truth?" Julian asked.

"Yes, I can see you're having trouble believing— what the smart folks call 'finding credibility in'—what I'm saying."

That proved it in Julian's eyes.

"OK. Fine. I believe you. You're me. I'm you. Whatever. Why are you here?"

"I need you to help me do something."

"What?"

"I kind of caused a problem. In the past."

"But you said you're from the future."

"I did. And I am."

"Then how did you cause a problem in the past?"

"It's complicated."

"So what do need me for?"

"I need your help changing history."

CHAPTER 6

"I must have hit my head. That's it. It's the only answer that makes any sense. I was sitting in the chair, and it fell over, and I bumped…" Julian stopped when he saw the chair standing upright. "Fine. No knock on the noggin. Then I'm dreaming. Yes, dreaming. I fell asleep while studying. And this is all a weird, though strangely lucid, dream. I know. I'll pinch myself and wake up. On the count of three. One…two…"

The stranger reached over and pinched his arm.

"Ow!" Julian yelped. "What did you do that for!"

"To save you the trouble."

"I didn't need your help."

"Don't get all riled up. What the smart folks call—"

"I KNOW WHAT RILED UP MEANS!"

"You don't have to yell. By the way, you'll outgrow that temper thing around fourteen, give or take. Anyway, let me restate my previous statement. I don't want to change history. I want to *un*-change history."

"Do I also outgrow talking in riddles?"

"I'm not getting you."

"Never mind." Even though it was still the afternoon, Julian suddenly felt ready to go to bed. "Go on."

"Have you figured out the clock thing yet? When he gave us the eTab, Dad told us what it's *supposed* to do. But have you found out what really happens?" Grown-up Julian asked.

Young Julian saw no sense in lying to himself.

"Well, it did some weird time...change...thing. On the way home yesterday. And I might have, sort of, just maybe, done a little bit of experimenting. Changing the clock, and all. But I have no idea *how* it works. Or why."

"Nobody does. Even Dad couldn't figure it out when I finally told him about it. But he and I both have tried our hands at tinkering with it. Upgrading it. Changing it," Grown-up Julian said, his voice losing volume and confidence with each word.

"Changing it how?"

"I thought that by adding some more numbers, and a second, inner circle with the numbers going backward, I could use it to..."

"What?"

"Travel forward and backward in time, as far as I want, in either direction. Well, that's not entirely true. The numbers go up to 199. So, 199 years, in either direction, is the most I can go."

"199 YEARS!"

"Yeah. Neat, huh?" Grown-up Julian said, clearly missing Young Julian's rising concern. "Let me tell you, Dad thinks it's really cool. So cool, in fact, that he put something like ten thousand numbers on his. He and Mom are vacationing in Pompeii right now and...Oh boy! I sure hope he remembers they're six hours ahead of us. Otherwise, it could be bad. Very bad. At least I think it could be bad. After all, I did miss a few of the classes, and was late for my final, and—"

"Classes? What classes?"

"Don't interrupt. It's very a rude habit. Unfortunately, you won't outgrow that one as successfully. Nor will you outgrow your freckles. But don't worry. You'll decide you like them the first time a girl tells you *she* likes them. Anyway, I'm no temporal scientist. Far from it. But I'm pretty sure it would have a negative impact on our very existence if Mom and Dad were to get buried under a mountain of lava two thousand years—"

"Since, apparently, I will never outgrow my rude habit of interrupting, I'm going to right now." Julian jumped in. "Let's not worry about Mom and Dad. They know how to take care of themselves. Well, Mom knows how to take care of herself and Dad. But you... me...us...No, *you* tinkered with the Dad Five-Minute Warning app. The app that somehow, for no apparent reason, throws people into the future? *You* tinkered with—"

"You're repeating yourself."

"Maybe now would be a good time for you to work on the interrupting thing."

"Point taken. Do you mind if I sit down? My legs are kind of tired. I did a lot of running today."

Young Julian pointed to the desk chair. Instead, his future self sat down on the floor, cross-legged. Young Julian joined him.

"The *point* is, don't you think changing the app was—"

"Stupid? What the smart folks call 'idiotic'?" Grown-up Julian said. "Probably. But I just had to."

"Actually, I was going to say 'unnecessary.' Why didn't you just change the calendar?"

"Why would I want to do that? The calendar worked just fine. Other than the event reminder sounding like a foghorn."

Though he was in the presence of a grown-up, Young Julian felt, somehow, as if he were the more mature one. It was like talking to Dad, version 2.0.

"No. I mean you...I...we...figured out that by setting the clock ahead 10 minutes, we could jump 16 minutes into the future."

"Yes. Yes, we did."

"Then I figured out you could open the calendar app, change the date, and use that as the jumping off point."

"Really? That works?"

"Yes, it...No, wait. I thought it might. But it was only a theory. I meant to test it out. But I didn't get to because I was—"

"Interrupted," they said in unison.

"Interesting," Grown-up Julian said, clearly contemplating the circularity of the whole thing. "In hindsight—or would that be foresight—I really wish I hadn't interrupted me today. Because if I hadn't, then

47

I might have gotten around to trying out our idea of changing the calendar, potentially saving me from having to re-jigger the Dad Five-Minute Warning app. *Now* I get what Professor Brown was talking about in that class I took last semester, Time-Interference Paradox 101."

"Speaking of which, what did you...we do? To mess up history?" Young Julian asked, glad he never actually took Step 5. With his luck, he probably would have wound up in a dinosaur's mouth.

"Well, we might not have."

"You're starting to make my head hurt."

"It's pretty simple, actually. I decided to go back to the Civil War. After all, we really love the Civil War, and—Do we love the Civil War yet?"

"We're just starting to study it in school."

"What do you think?"

"It seems kind of boring, especially when compared to some other wars. The ones with real weapons."

"Real weapons?"

"You know, like tanks and bombers and submarines."

"I do recall thinking that, yes. No worries. Just wait. Your...our opinion will change. And trust me. Cannons and guns are real weapons. I know, because I went back to Gettysburg. *The* battle, after all, right? And while I was back there, in 1863, watching it all, I might have dropped my cell phone somewhere."

"Excuse me? You did what?"

"OK. I dropped my...our cell phone. Boy, this me-you-us thing is getting confusing. Tell you what.

From now on, I'll say 'me,' when referring to me," he said, index finger pointed at his chest, "and you say 'you.' Deal?"

"Deal."

"Now, where was I?"

"In Gettysburg. About to be stupid."

"You don't have to be snippy about it, Young Me. I was at Gettysburg, being *curious*. And *inquisitive*. And I just happened to drop my phone. In a field. Somewhere. In 1863."

"Who were you calling?"

"What? No one. Why?"

"I'm just trying to figure out why you decided you needed to place a call, like, ten years before Alexander Graham Bell invented the telephone."

"News flash. Cell phones do more than just make phone calls, Caveboy."

"Now *you* can stop being snippy."

"Fine. I promise."

"I guess we don't outgrow *that,*" Young Julian groused.

Grown-up Julian answered only with a guilty-as-charged shrug.

"So you lost your cell phone. Big deal. Dad used to do it, like, three times a day. At least before he invented the Shirt Phone," Young Julian said, unconcerned, owing to the fact that he had not yet taken Time-Interference Paradox 101.

"Oh! I wish I'd remembered about the Shirt Phone. It would have saved me the trouble of...all this."

Grown-up Julian waved his hands around in a vaguely situation-encompassing manner. "No offense."

"None taken. So, get another one."

"It's not that simple. Well, yes, it is, as far as getting another phone is concerned. But that's not the problem. The problem is, if someone finds it, it could completely change history as we know it."

"Change history? How?"

"No one can say. We won't know until it happens. It might make 'today' better. Or not."

"This is unbelievable. How could you drop your phone?"

"Well, I was off to one side. Hiding behind a tree, much like any rational but unarmed person would do on a historic battlefield. Then Pickett's Charge started. *The* turning point of the battle and, ultimately, the war. How cool is that? I'm standing there, watching Pickett's Charge. History was unfolding before my eyes," Grown-up Julian said, his eyes finding that faraway place Young Julian often witnessed his dad viewing wistfully. "I just had to take a picture. But then bullets started flying. I tucked the phone in my pocket and ran. At least, I thought I tucked it in my pocket. I know I ran. But when I checked, it was—"

"No. I mean, how could you be so clumsy?"

"Trust me, we are."

Great, Young Julian thought. *Another thing I have to look forward to.*

"Well, what do you think you should..." said Young Julian. He stopped and looked around. "Hold on. Everything today is normal."

Grown-up Julian looked around, too. "If you insist."

"The point is, history hasn't been changed. So, they didn't find it."

"No. They just didn't find it yet."

"What do you mean? It's in the past. More than a hundred years ago."

"*More than* a hundred years ago? Nothing like a little ballpark figure."

"I told you, we just started studying it. The point is, it happened. Or, it didn't happen."

"No. It's hard to explain. To be honest, I don't understand all the details—what the smart folks call 'intricacies'—of time travel. Like I said, before you interrupted, I did take a course on it. At the community college. But I missed a few classes. Time is kind of a continuous looping thing. So, as we speak, some guy with those big bushy sideburns that meet up with his mustache might be picking it up, and saying 'WTF,' or whatever they said back then. Or, maybe history *has* changed. But you don't realize it, because everything else over the past 150-plus years—everything leading up to this moment—has changed. But *if* everything has changed, it wasn't supposed to. And that could have unintended consequences."

"Unintended consequences? Like what?"

"Worst case, the universe could end prematurely."

"WHAT!?"

"Chill out. Like I said, it's a *worst*-case scenario. More likely, any premature demise would be limited to the Earth. The solar system, tops."

"I feel so much better. Now here's a wacky idea. Go back and get it. Problem solved."

"I don't have enough charge."

"You what?"

"My eTab is almost out of juice."

"So why did you come here? Now?"

"What?"

"Why did you come here, instead of going back to your own time, charging it up, then going back to the Civil War?"

The question made perfect sense to Young Julian, even though nothing else about the last fifteen minutes did.

"I didn't have enough charge to go all the way there, either. Back to my time. I only had enough to get here. Time travel requires a lot of power. Traveling farther takes more power."

"If you insist. So once you realized you'd dropped it, why not just go back to a few minutes before?"

"See that? We're smart. Always thinking. Your idea does look good on paper. But there are two little flaws in your budding logic."

"Only two?"

"For now. One. The bullets were flying. My only thought was *Get me the heck out of the Civil War*. Not *Hey, why don't I go farther back into it*. Two. If I had jumped back twenty minutes, it would have used up even more of the charge, potentially stranding me there forever. Or at least until a future me decided to go back to find me and... Well, I'm sure you see where this is heading."

"Wow. This is hard. We're really going to understand all this?"

"Define 'understand.' The point is, when I did the calculations—we'll be very good at math, by the way—I realized I had enough charge to get to *now*, but not ten years from now."

"Eight years."

"Right. Eight years. And, I thought, who better to help me than me!"

"If that's all you need, I'll just—Hmmm. I never did ask Dad how to charge it. But, it shouldn't be a problem. I'll just ask him for the charger, bring it up here, plug it in, and then you'll be fine."

"Ummm..."

Even at the age of twelve, Julian knew that "Ummm" rarely was followed by something positive, like "Great idea!"

"Ummm what?" Young Julian sighed.

"We don't plug things in, in the future. We just put in power cells."

"What are power cells?"

"They're like batteries."

"Fine. We have batteries."

"Not like these. They're the size of...quarters... Yes," he said, thinking for a moment, "quarters do still exist. Now, today, at least."

"What do you mean?"

"Money is a lot different in the future. But that's beside the point. The point is, they're not like regular batteries. You plug them in...here," Grown-up Julian said as he pointed to a place on the front. They last for like a year, and then you replace them."

"What's inside of them?"

"Cucumium, I think. Or was it Bubumium? No, Bubumium's the stuff I invented in eleventh grade to mimic the symptoms of bubonic plague. Really effective for getting out of class. I could have made a mint on that, selling it to the other kids at school, especially the day before Senior Cut Day. If Dad hadn't confiscated it. Nope, it must be Cucumium."

"Cucumium? What's that?"

"I don't know. It's some kind of chemical. Or mineral. I don't think it's an animal or a vegetable. You really need to pay better attention in Mr. Beaker's eleventh grade chemistry class, instead of concocting your own devious samples of elementary matter."

"Fine. Mental note: no devious samples of elementary matter in Mr. Somebody's eleventh grade chemistry class. Back to our problem. How do we get this Cu—"

"Cucumium. The same way we get everything. We just tell the replicator 'I need a new power cell.' And there it is."

"Really?" Young Julian asked, amazed—what the smart folks call "agog."

"No, not really. That's *Star Trek*."

Young Julian frowned. "So, where do you get it, or them?"

"The same place we get everything. GoogMart."

"GoogMart? I've never heard of it."

"Because it doesn't exist yet."

"Then what do we do?"

"Dad's an inventor. So we just need to figure out how to get him to invent it. Soon. Really soon. Really, really soon."

"Why soon?"

"Well, I think there might be a teeny, tiny, eensie, weensie microscopic possibility that if the power cell totally dies, it could erase the eTab's memory, including the upgraded clock app."

"WHAT!?"

"I said, it might...*might*... totally erase the eTab's memory, including the Dad Five-Minute Warning app."

"Which would?"

"Strand me here permanently."

"Permanently?"

"Afraid so."

"But wait. You could change the calendar. That works."

"Or not. It's really too bad you didn't get to actually try out the theory."

"Yeah. Pity," Young Julian said, flexing his still nascent sarcasm muscles. "Any other news you want to share?"

"No. That's about it."

"Fine. Look, since my eTab is at ninety-five percent," Young Julian said, more than a hint of techno-smugness in his voice, "maybe we can somehow use it to help you get back to your time. Let's think about it after—"

"Dinner time!" his mom called up.

"Ooh! I'm hungry. Really hungry," Grown-up Julian said. "I didn't eat before I left. And I smell broccoli. I *love* broccoli! Do you think you could get me a plate?"

"That it? Anything else?"

"Yeah. If Mom or Dad bring up Pompeii, change the subject."

CHAPTER 7

"I'm so glad you all decided to attend," Mr. Newcomber said, launching dinner with his official (and officially worn out) joke.

The Newcomber family had two firm rules with regard to dinner. (Aside from the obvious ones, like no throwing food and no sitting in the wrong chairs.)

Rule #1. Dinner was required—what the smart folks call "mandatory," and the really wise ones call "you darned better well be there."

Rule #2. Everybody had to talk about his or her day.

There was one more rule, courtesy of Mrs. Newcomber—whom Mr. Newcomber smartly called "The Boss." None of Mr. Newcomber's inventions were permitted at the table.

Julian's dad cleared his throat and continued. "Normally, I work very hard to contain my enthusiasm, deferring to you, my beloved children. But I just *have* to go first. This might surprise you, but I invented something today."

Julian noticed his mom getting ready in case his dad violated the no inventions rule.

"I'm tired of all the floors in this old house creaking and squeaking when even a mouse walks across them. This," Mr. Newcomber said, holding up what looked like a toothpaste tube, only the size of a jumbo, extra-grande burrito, "will stop it. I call it No Squeak, an obvious play on my mouse comment of just…Never mind. I wanted to call it Sssssh! But the American Association of Librarians has trademarked that word and threatened legal action. Quietly, of course."

"I'm not sure I like that idea," said Mrs. Newcomber. "If the floors don't creak I won't hear you sneaking up on me. Which you have a habit of doing."

"Is it really that much of an issue?" he asked.

Mom gave him the patented (or maybe it was trademarked) look that said without words, "Yes, it is."

"Then…Maybe you should put bells on all my shoes. That way you'll hear me coming," said Mr. Newcomber.

Julian did not notice his mother's raised eyebrow, the gesture she made when planning—what the smart folks call "diabolically plotting"—something.

"So, Julian," Mrs. Newcomber asked, "how was your day?"

"Interesting," said Julian, an answer he felt told the truth. Just not all of it.

"What new and exciting thing did you learn today?" Mr. Newcomber asked. He was always interested in the new and the exciting.

"We're starting to study the Civil War," Julian said.

"The Civil Way, eh? That is interesting. Maybe some time we should take a long weekend and visit one of the battlefields. Like, Gettysburg, perhaps. You'd probably enjoy seeing it, Julian."

If you only knew, Julian thought. "I probably would."

"Oh, if only I were a teacher. The homework projects I could come up with..."

"Andrew..." Mrs. Newcomber said in that special way of hers which lengthened—what the smart folks call "elongated"—every syllable and told Mr. Newcomber he'd best stop talking.

Julian interjected so as to save his father from, yet again, having to "yes dear" his way out of another mess-in-the-making. "There's a project. I have to do a diorama. About the battle of Gettysburg, actually."

"A diorama!" Mr. Newcomber said, bouncing in his seat. "I could *so* help you with it. I'll bet without too much effort I could make up some miniature cannons. And maybe even—"

"Andrew..." said Mrs. Newcomber, stretching out his name even more, for a good five seconds, though to Mr. Newcomber it probably felt like eight minutes.

"But honey! It would be so—"

Julian's mom shot a look across the table that would have made General Pickett yell "Retreat!"

"OK," Mr. Newcomber said in a quiet, if not subdued and slightly dejected, voice. "It's just that Gettysburg is so interesting. It was the turning point of the war. And it lasted three days. Three days! Oh, what I wouldn't give to be able to see it."

His dad got *that* look in his eyes. And Julian realized where he (the other he) got the idea to use the eTab to surf through time.

Mr. Newcomber continued, "You know another place I would love to see firsthand? Pom–"

"Tell us about your day, Dylan," Julian said quickly—what the smart folks call "hastily."

"We had library today," said Dylan.

"Library day always was my favorite," said Mrs. Newcomber, who to this day still read about five books each afternoon. "What did you get?"

"I got a book called *Zombies in Nature*."

"Dylan!" Olivia chided. "Zombies aren't real!"

"Oho!" Mr. Newcomber said, "But indeed they are. Many creepie-crawlies have evolved some devious method for taking over some other hapless creature. For example, there is a fungus that infects ants, feeding on their organs. Sloooooowly. But it saves the brain for last, and since the host is an ant, the brain's little more than a snack. Once the fungus has nearly drained the unfortunate *Formicidae*, it works the poor thing's brain like a puppet master, forcing the ant to climb a blade of grass. Having attained a sufficient altitude, relatively speaking, the spores that had been festering inside the ant explode and—"

"Andrew," his mother said evenly, as she always did, "perhaps you could find a more palatable, shall we say 'less grotesque,' topic of conversation for the dinner table."

Though his mother opened with "perhaps," Julian fully understood she was not making a suggestion.

"So, Dylan, did you get any other books today?"

"I also got one on King Arthur."

"Oooh," gushed Mr. Newcomber. "King Arthur. Camelot. The Knights of the Round Table. Another really interesting place in time to visit, as long as one is prepared to be disappointed, as it most likely is fict—"

"Mommy! Daddy!" Olivia broke in, saving Julian the trouble of having to find another way to redirect his dad's attention. "Did you hear what Dylan did at recess? He—"

"No I didn't," Dylan interrupted.

"Yes you did."

"Did not!"

"Did!"

"DID NOT!"

"DID!"

Exchanges—what the realistic folks call "inane arguments"—between Dylan and Olivia could go on for hours. At minimum, Julian hoped it would last long enough to make his dad completely forget about visiting other places and, more importantly, other times.

Mrs. Newcomber snapped her fingers so loudly the chandelier shook and the curtains moved in the breeze created by the shock wave, a talent Julian felt rivaled the homemaking thing. Once the echoes faded away, silence returned to the table.

"Much better," said Mrs. Newcomber. "So far, it sounds as though everyone had a pretty good day.

This warms my heart. Really. I mean that, kids. I hear so many parents talking to each other about the messes their children are making. So, it makes me very happy to know everyone is growing, in all the right ways. And learning."

Mrs. Newcomber had a way of bringing peace to any household battlefield. Julian often thought she probably could just as easily convince warring nations to lay down their arms.

Perhaps she *should go back to the Civil War*, Julian thought.

"Now, tell us about your day, Olivia."

"In Shop class I designed and built a combination microwave-convection-conventional oven. I call it the Insta-Cake Bake. Then, in Home Ec., I used it to make a chocolate angel food cake."

"I assume you used Grandma's secret recipe?"

"Yup."

"That's my girl."

Olivia and Mrs. Newcomber performed their secret "girls-only" handshake ritual, which by now took nearly one minute, and required digital contortions Julian had thought not possible.

"Constructing and cooking. Just like your mother. Combining two amazing—Wait a minute. Did you say an angel food cake?"

"Yes, Daddy."

"But angel food cakes are this big," he said, holding his hands about a foot apart.

"More like," Olivia replied, holding hers about two feet apart.

"That's one humongous cake," said Mr. Newcomber.

"You know I came from a big family," said Mrs. Newcomber. "Grandma always cooked everything in massive quantities."

"So that would have to be one mighty big oven you built," Mr. Newcomber said, smiling at his daughter.

Olivia just shrugged.

"Impressive, Peanut. Very impressive."

Olivia smiled broadly—what the smart folks call "beamed." She liked it when her daddy called her by her pet name.

"Impressive, Peanut," Dylan said in an annoying, bordering on needling, voice.

Olivia did *not* like it when her brother borrowed their dad's pet name for her. "Shut up, Dylan."

"Olivia," Mrs. Newcomber said, stern of voice.

"But Mommy!" Olivia whined.

"'But Mommy' nothing."

"But he started it."

"But he started it," Dylan said in full-on mocking tone again.

"Mommy!"

"I don't care if he started it," said Mrs. Newcomber. "You do not tell him to shut up."

"Yeah, Peanut!" Dylan said.

"And you," Mrs. Newcomber said, focusing her laser-beam eyes on Dylan, "you will, one, not taunt your sister, and two, *not* taunt your sister. Do I make myself clear?"

"Yes, Mama."

"Hah!" said Olivia.

"Mama!" Dylan shouted.

"Olivia." Mrs. Newcomber repeated, a decibel or two louder.

"But he started it."

The process threatened to resume and, more likely than not, simply repeat itself. In some cases, the "Shut up"/"Mama / Mommy!"/"He started it" verbal volleyball match had been known to go through a dozen or so cycles—what the smart folks call "iterations."

Mr. Newcomber held up what looked like a large garage door opener, albeit one with two large rabbit-ear antennas sticking out of the top. Painted on the back were the words Attention Getter, underscoring Mr. Newcomber's love of naming his creations. He pushed a button on the Attention Getter, a clear violation of the no inventions rule. The thing hummed a minute. Then a spark of electricity emerged from the top, at the very bottom of the rabbit-ear V, and traveled up, up, up. When it reached the end, a thunderous boom filled the room. The crack preceded a sizzling sound that reverberated through the room and perhaps as far as low Earth orbit. The lights above the dining room table flickered, faded, then went out. From where he sat, Julian could see the entire neighborhood had gone black as well.

"Andrew?" said Mrs. Newcomber. This time she spoke in short syllables, which meant Julian's dad was in a different kind of trouble.

"Hmmm," Mr. Newcomber said. "That wasn't supposed to happen."

A few minutes later, dining by candlelight, Julian sat, present in body only, his fork tracing circles, squares, and parallelograms on the plate. Though the typical Newcomber dinnertime circus offered some degree of diversion, even this latest installment of the Dylan-Olivia Comedy Hour could not let him completely forget, even for a moment, that a future version of himself sat upstairs, hungry and stranded in the wrong year. In fact, so distracted was Julian that he didn't hear his mother ask him—three times—if he wanted more mashed potatoes.

"No, thank you. Wait. Yes, please. And I'd like a large helping of broccoli, too."

"You would?" said Mrs. Newcomber.

"Yeah. Why? What?"

"You hate broccoli."

"I do hate...um...I mean I *used* to hate it. But now I've decided I really like it. So, I'd like some. A lot."

"If you insist." She heaped a massive quantity of *ewww* on his plate.

After a few minutes of staring at the offensive green weed and dreading the prospect of having to actually eat it, Julian excused himself to use the bathroom. He didn't really have to go. He just needed to spend some time away from his plate so he wouldn't get sick from looking at, and thinking about, and smelling the vile vegetable, the bane of children and devout carnivores everywhere. Also, he wanted to give his mom and dad and brother and sister enough time to finish their dinners and leave the table, so he could sneak back, grab his plate, and take it up to his room.

Twelve minutes later, he placed the plate in front of Grown-up Julian, who was sitting in the dark with a flashlight on.

"An invention gone wrong—what the smart folks call 'awry'?" Grown-up Julian asked, basking in the flashlight's glow.

"What do you think?" said Young Julian.

"He violated the no inventions rule, huh?"

"Yup. By the way, I hope you appreciate this sacrifice on my part."

"Oh, I do!" said Grown-up Julian. "This is great. I love Mom's cooking."

"No. I mean I hope you appreciate the lie I had to tell get the broccoli. I told Mom I love it now. So, she's probably going to make it three times a week. Six, if you count the breakfast smoothies. Thanks a lot. Why couldn't your favorite food be peanut butter?"

"Hey, don't blame me for the fact that you can't tell a good lie."

"What do you mean?"

"What you should have said was, 'I'd like to *try* broccoli again, Mom.' Then take one bite and then say, 'Nah, I still don't like it.' Then you would have had an excuse to leave it on your plate. Besides, what's the big deal? You will love broccoli. Someday."

"You know, you need to stop doing this."

"Which this?"

"Telling me about the future. You're spoiling it."

"Look, 95.8% of kids hate broccoli. And guess

what? 99.9% will like it as adults. So, I see nothing wrong with pointing out the obvious. Though, I suppose a bigger issue is that I could be polluting the natural timeline."

"Polluting the what?"

"Polluting the timeline. It's something they talked about in that class. Though, if memory serves, I think I bombed the quiz on that topic as well. No matter. Like I said before dinner, if someone from 1863 finds my cell phone, it will alter history, assuming he doesn't just throw it out. Telling you about the future probably is the same thing. Would anything I tell you make the future better or worse? No one can say. It's just that changing time is bad."

"How bad?"

"I don't know. It's not like they gave us any time-line-altering homework assignments. Or lab exercises. Or field trips. Or—"

"I get it."

"I suspect they didn't want to give us any stupid ideas."

"You think? I wish you had listened to me."

"What?"

"Remember? In the library the other day? The vow I took? We took? The vow to never go back in time? What about that?"

"What about the vow you took—*you* took—to never hit Dylan?"

"I stopped. Didn't I?"

"Yeah. But not until he got bigger than you."

"Wait! Dylan gets bigger than me?"

"Yup. And that's not all. He—"

"Stop it! You know, we've really got to come up with some ground rules about this. About your spoilers."

"Ground away."

Young Julian thought, in the absence of his older version doing so. *Ever*, it seemed.

"OK. If it's a matter of life or death, tell me. Otherwise, ix-nay on the abbing-blay. Do we have a deal?" Young Julian said, extending his hand.

"Yeah. Sort of. But no promises."

"What? No. You need to pinky swear."

"Can't."

"Why not?"

"How would you grade your current level of impulse control? Specifically, your ability to hold your tongue and not blab out whatever comes to mind, regardless of who is speaking, or watching a really good movie."

"I would give myself an A..."

Grown-up Julian looked funny at his junior self.

"...a grade of B minus or so."

"'Nuff said. Don't tell me anything else about my future. I just want to be clear—what the smart folks call...'CRYSTAL CLEAR'!"

"Point taken. Oh! But there is one thing you do need to know."

"What?"

"Make sure you tell Dad to—"

"Wait! Are you trying to...what did you call it? Pollute the natural timeline?"

"No! Of course not! Don't be silly. Well, OK. Yes.

But it's no big deal. It's not like it will change the course of human history if I let you know—"

Young Julian put his fingers in his ears, and sang, "La la la. I can't hear you!"

So he did not hear Grown-up Julian say, "Tell Dad to sell all of his Apple stock. In a few years, they're going to come out with iHam. It's going to be a huge flop. The company will tank. If he sells now and banks the money, I...*you* won't need to take out any loans for college."

When Grown-up Julian's lips stopped moving, Young Julian took his fingers out of his ears.

"Are you done?" Young Julian asked.

"You really should have listened. If you had, you wouldn't be getting that job at the pizza place."

"I said life or death!"

"Have you ever worked at a pizza parlor?"

"I'm twelve, I can't get a job yet. Besides, I like pizza. And I don't like the thought of being responsible for messing up the future. Capisce?"

"Caposh."

"Heh-heh. We do say that."

From the other side of Julian's door came a sound. Faint, at first, it grew louder. *Thump thump thump thump thump* THUMP THUMP THUMP THUMP

It should have grown quieter.

THUMP THUMP THUMP THUMP

But it did not. It stopped at its loudest.

"Uh-oh," both Julians said simultaneously.

The door flew open, and in flew Dylan, a barely contained ball of excitement on his calm days.

"Julian! Julian! You'll never believe what I just built and—"

Seeing Grown-up Julian immediately shut Dylan up, something Young Julian wished he could do on demand. Dylan's mouth dropped open, and his eyes grew as big as saucers.

"I think we're in trouble—what the smart folks call 'up a creek without—'"

Dylan found his voice. "MMMMMOOOOOOOMMMMMMM!" he screamed as he ran from the room.

"We're dead. She'll be here any second now," Young Julian said.

"Nah. We have forty-five seconds. Or more," Grown-up Julian said.

"What"

"It will take Dylan at least twenty seconds to find Mom. Another ten to explain it to her. And then fifteen for her to get here."

"How do you know?"

"Experience, Young Me. Experience."

"Maybe we should just come clean."

"You really think that's a good idea?"

"Sure. Maybe she can help us."

"Julian!" his mother called as the first hurried footsteps reached their ears.

"Or not," Grown-up Julian said.

"Come on. This is *our* mom. What hasn't she seen after all these years with Dad? I'm sure she won't even blink."

"You think?"

"OK. She might blink. She might even scream.

Once. Two, three, ten times, tops. But really, what's the worst thing that could happen?"

"Has Dad told you about any of those anti-burglar inventions he came up with yet? Has he even invented them yet? Like the Remote Controlled Nunchucks or the Mace-Laced Pants or—"

"Say no more. What are we going to do?"

"I'm going to hide."

"Where?"

"Out here." Grown-up Julian slid open the window and stepped out onto the roof of the front porch.

"Are you sure that's safe?"

The meter of the footsteps increased to eighty beats per minute.

"Totally," Grown-up Julian said, sticking his head back in the window.

"How do you know?"

"Because in a few years, *you'll* know."

"I don't think I want to know."

"You probably don't, Young Me."

"What am I going to tell Mom?"

"You'll think of something. We're smart."

Grown-up Julian gave the thumbs-up and slid the casement back down, barely rustling the curtains in the process. Young Julian suspected that sooner, rather than later, he would develop the same skill. The approaching footsteps now could be mistaken for a tap-dancing recital. Julian dashed across to his desk, deposited himself in the chair, and opened the nearest textbook. Which just happened to be a Spanish book. Last year's Spanish book, to be more precise. Last year's Spanish book, upside down, to be exact.

Against—what the smart folks call "contrary to"—the Newcomber house rules, his mom didn't bother knocking before bursting into the room. Of course, neither had Dylan, which started this whole mess. Her eyes were as big as *bigger* saucers.

"Hi, Mom," Julian said coolly. "Is everything OK?"

She wasn't answering. She was looking.

And looking.

And looking.

"Mom?"

"Your brother said he saw a man in here."

"A man? In here?"

"Yes. A man. In here."

"Hmmm. A man, in here," Julian said as he walked over and stood by her side, following her eyes as they scanned the room. He wanted to be ready with an answer—what the honest folks call "a fabrication"—in case she spotted something unusual. Relatively speaking, that is. "Do *you* see anyone else in here, Mom?"

Julian assumed she could not see Grown-up Julian outside. But sometimes it seemed as though his mom had super powers. And Superman could see through walls. So, he wasn't taking any chances.

"No."

"Good. I don't either. I think I'll just get back to my..." he said, taking a small and subtle sidestep toward the desk.

But his mom was not leaving. She was still looking.

And looking.

And looking.

"He was sure, Julian. He didn't say, 'I thought I saw.' He said, 'I *saw*.' Are you certain there's—"

Julian considered blaming television, too much sugar, and an over-active imagination, a strategy all parents fell back on when they had no better ideas. Instead, he offered up the most convenient and reasonable explanation, fingers crossed, hoping it actually approached plausible.

"Isn't Dad working on an invention, a toy called Not-Invisible Invisible Friend or something like that?" His dad was not, at least as far as Julian knew. But he knew his mom would not know either.

"A what?"

"A Not-Invisible Invisible Friend." Julian fought the question mark his brain was trying really hard to add to the end of the sentence.

"I can never be sure," his mom said, her voice sounding both tired and frustrated—what the smart folks call "exasperated." Julian suspected her answer would be something along those lines.

"I'm pretty sure he is. That's probably what Dylan saw."

"I suppose," she said, taking one last look around. "I need to have a talk with my husband."

Julian knew that when his mom called his dad "my husband," he was in big trouble.

"Well," his mom continued, "don't let me be the excuse for your homework not getting done."

"Never. Bye, Mom."

Julian knew to not say a word until he *heard* the footsteps retreating. (Though he had no proof, Julian suspected his mom had asked his dad to invent a highly classified sound-making device which, if it really did exist and had a name, that name would be something like Honest, I'm Walking Away Now.) Apparently, Grown-up Julian suspected it too, as he waited a good minute before stepping back in.

"That was great, Young Me."

"I hate lying to Mom."

"I know," Grown-up Julian mumbled in a way that said—what the smart folks call "conveyed"—he had done it often and regretted it each time.

The two sat in silence for a minute. Finally, Young Julian spoke.

"I'll try to outgrow the lying to Mom thing as well. OK?"

"OK. Say, Young Me, what time is it?"

"9:00."

"It's late," said Grown-up Julian. "Well, not really. But time travel takes a lot out of you. I'm beat. Dibs on the upper bunk."

"No way!"

"But I called it. And I'm older."

"Yeah, but I live here and you don't. You don't...do you? Still live here?"

"No. But Mom and Dad do."

"Really? That has to be some kind of record."

"Tell me about it. I think Mom's less-than-subtle suggestion—a.k.a. mandate—that Dad put his lab out in the back yard, instead of the basement, made all the difference in the world."

"I'm glad to hear it. I really like it here. This house. This town."

"Whispering Falls *is* nice. Listen, this really won't ruin anything. You're going to make a lot of good friends here. You'll do fine. Just give yourself some time."

"Thanks."

Grown-up Julian then faked—what the smart folks call "feigned"—a great big yawn, followed by a stretch.

"Well, it's getting late," he said. "I'll just..."

"Forget it," said Young Julian, blocking his path to the ladder. "You can't have the top bunk."

"Rock, paper, scissors?"

"Nope."

"Flip a coin?"

"No. I'm sleeping up top. And that's final."

Grown-up Julian snorted a little. "I don't remember being such a stubborn kid."

CHAPTER 8

The next morning, after breakfast and before his walk to school, Young Julian felt he had to go over things with Grown-up Julian.

"What are you going to do today? While I'm at school."

"Maybe I'll go over to the library, and—It's still there, right?"

"It is."

"Of course it is. You were just there, experimenting," Grown-up Julian said, tapping his temple to emphasize that he still remembered a few details from his youth. "I loved that place. So I'll go use one of their computers to surf the web. See if I can find something, anything from today that might relate to Cucumium. I think I still remember how to use a keyboard," Grown-up Julian

"There are no keyboards? At all?"

"Nope, we use—"

"Don't tell me!"

"Ooh! But there is something I do need to tell you."

"What?"

"Remember this. It's important. At least it will be, in the future. You need to—"

"Forget it." Young Julian grabbed his pillow and wrapped it around his head, muffling Grown-up Julian saying, "Don't bother asking Darla Bratt to the senior prom. She'll just spend the night hanging all over Brian Borden. Instead, you should ask Linda Burg. Her dad is going to invent inflatable yogurt, and they'll be gazillionaires."

When Grown-up Julian's lips had stopped moving, Young Julian tossed the pillow back on the bed.

"Are you done?"

"You really need to start listening to me."

"Not a chance. Oh, and don't forget. Dad works in the backyard."

"Oh, right. I suppose I'd better not go for a walk around the yard then. Hmmm. The kitchen might be dangerous as well. After all, he does snack. Do you think maybe, just maybe, before you leave you could..." he said, looking sad—what the smart folks call "pathetic"—and rubbing his stomach.

"I'm late for school."

"But I'll be hungry!"

"Better get your replicator to make your lunch. See ya."

Young Julian walked the half-mile down Washington, then just past Philomethian Street (a name chosen, no doubt, to make spelling tests seem easier in comparison), and turned right on the sandstone sidewalk leading up to the three-story brick school. As he passed some kids on the playground, he remembered his mother's advice, though based on her tone of voice, Julian took it to be *his* mandate: "Try to make some friends."

He would, he promised himself. Soon. Just not today.

Julian joined the crowd—what the smart folks call "the throng"—milling around the front door. He moved strategically, maneuvering to the base of the stone steps. When the "bussers" arrived and began streaming across the playground, the front doors swung open, and the mass moved inside. Experience had taught Julian that he needed to be near some other sixth graders when the inward surge started. Otherwise, he might find himself swept up to the third floor with the fourth graders, unable to swim free of the tide of preteen humanity.

Julian just managed to catch the railing at Floor Two and pull himself from the upward flow. He deposited the textbooks for his afternoon classes in his locker and took his seat in homeroom. Looking around, he watched his classmates and felt a slight sense of jealousy. Every one of them was engaged in a conversation. Some juggled two. He studied their faces. They were happy, carefree. Julian took comfort—what the smart folks call "solace"—in the words his future self had said last night: "You're going to make a lot of good friends here. You'll do fine."

Unfortunately, today he could not be happy. And the concept of carefree felt miles away.

"Class, please put away your books, and take out a pencil," Mrs. Stern said. "We are having a pop quiz."

Hearing the groans, you would have thought she had said, "You will all be getting flu shots, then force-fed brussels sprouts."

Julian accepted the page that Lisa Honey...something, the girl who sat at the desk ahead of his, handed him. He thought for a happy second she might have, possibly, perhaps, maybe, smiled at him. A little bit. Even better, he was fairly certain he successfully smiled back.

He dove into the quiz and began working the problems. Math was one of his best subjects. Truth be told, he enjoyed most of them. Except for gym, since Biff clearly thought of Julian as his personal moving dodgeball target. And Biff could fling a ball with the best of them. Julian was fairly certain the marks dotting the gym wall—perfect six-inch circles where the paint had been knocked off—were Biff's work. (They reminded Julian of crop circles, those rural oddities—what the smart folks call "phenomena"—thought to be the work of aliens, and later discovered to be the work of teenagers bored with cow-tipping.) *I wonder if Dad could invent invisible body armor for me to wear under my gym uniform,* Julian thought with a shudder as he imagined the menacing scowl Biff always sported during dodgeball. *I'll have to ask Dad about it at dinner to—*

"All right, class. Put your pencils down, and hand your tests forward."

Just as Julian let go of his page, he noticed every answer was the same: 199.

Julian sighed and put his head down on the desk.

CHAPTER 9

After math class came science. He shuffled down to the lab, and wondered whether Mr. Nitro would simply lecture, or truly entertain them with some wacky demonstration. In that sense—what the smart folks call "regard"—Mr. Nitro reminded Julian of his father, though as far as Julian knew, Mr. Nitro never blew up a school and had to move across several state lines to find a new job. *He and Dad should get together some time and chat*, Julian thought, immediately discarding the idea upon noticing that Mr. Nitro's hair looked a little frizzier today, perhaps due to an earlier experiment gone wrong.

"Good morning, young scientists" Mr. Nitro began. (Mr. Nitro always referred to them as young scientists.) "Today we will continue our exploration of the periodic table with an in-depth look at..." The ever-enthusiastic teacher threw a bunch of pennies on the Money Magnifier (one of *his* fickle gizmos) casting the images of an equal number of manhole-cover-sized cents on the ceiling. "—Oops. My aim is a little off—" He adjusted the projector to point at the front wall. "...an in-depth look at copper! Copper is one of only four metals that, in its natural, elemental form, is a color other than gray or silver. Your lone homework assignment for the rest of the semester is to name the other three."

Twenty-five pencils began scribbling quickly—what the smart folks call "furiously."

"JUST KIDDING!"

Twenty-five voices said, "*Awww!*"

"But I will give you ten bonus points on your next test—whenever *that* may be—if you name them. Where were we? Oh yes! Copper. Atomic number twenty-nine. Its symbol is..." He pointed to the proper square on the large periodic table behind him. "...Cu."

Cu?! Julian thought, and nearly yelled. "Cu," he said slightly aloud, as a choir of angelic voices washed through his ears. (Of course, Mr. Nitro's class was next to the music room. So no surprise that Julian often heard singing in there.)

Mr. Nitro's lips continued to move. But Julian heard no words. Just two letters:

Cu.

Cu.

Cu! Cu! Cu! Cu!

Julian felt fairly certain Mr. Nitro was not repeating himself, nor "stuck in a groove," like those funny black, round plates that his dad still somehow made music come out of sometimes did.

Julian tried to listen carefully to Mr. Nitro's lesson.

But his brain kept saying, *Cu...Cucumium...Cu...Cucumium...Angels singing. It's a sign.*

He wrestled with—and lost to—temptation. He had to know.

Julian pulled the eTab from his backpack, rolled it open, and set it in his lab book. He had just called up the search engine when an ominous hand eclipsed the screen.

"Thank you," Mr. Nitro said, relieving Julian of the eTab. Luckily it had a snap-flat feature, so when laid out it looked like most other tablets. Otherwise, Mr. Nitro, ever curious, might have tried to take it apart.

A whole boatload of emotions—sadness, embarrassment, panic—washed over Julian as Mr. Nitro carried the eTab to the front of the room. That boatload capsized and quickly sank when Mr. Nitro placed it in his desk drawer, locked it, and pocketed the key.

Julian spent the next thirty-two minutes working on a deep, sincere apology and the exact words he would use to ask Mr. Nitro to give back the eTab, hoping a good job on the former would make the latter not necessary.

Why thirty-two minutes?

Because with three minutes left to go before the bell, Mr. Nitro sneezed. At first, it was a small *achoo.* The next was a little louder. The third actually made the overhead light fixtures sway in the breeze. He followed up this trio of nose explosions with a tremendous honk into his plaid handkerchief.

After another honk, he looked at the class with watery eyes and wheezed, "I'm sorry—" *ACHOC!* "—young scientists, but I'm afraid my—" HONK! "—allergies are acting up. Class dismissed."

ACH-HONK!

Mr. Nitro hurried out the door.

Twenty-four voices yelled, "YAAAY!"

One did not.

Could this day get any worse? Julian wondered.

The English paper that somehow failed to upload from Google Docs, the overdue library book he'd forgotten at home, the mystery meat at lunch that Julian swore crawled off his tray when he wasn't looking, and the body check Biff somehow managed to work into the rope climb during gym class answered the question. So all in all the day turned out just peachy.

When the bell rang, Julian pretended it was his alarm clock waking him from the horrible dream this day had been. He mentally put on his comfy robe and his fuzzy slippers and trudged down the hall, hoping a nice breakfast would be waiting for him.

Neither eggs nor oatmeal greeted him as he stepped outside. On a positive note, neither did Biff.

Julian knew he probably should have gone straight home. Too much unexpected, unexplainable, out-of-the-ordinary, bizarre stuff had happened in the last twenty-four hours, and none of it the usual kind of unexpected, unexplainable, out-of-the-ordinary, bizarre stuff he had grown accustomed to. He needed a break from it all, and his new favorite after-school spot called out to him. (It didn't *really* call out to him, in the echoing-through-the-schoolyard sense; that's just what the smart folks say when speaking of something alluring, enticing, or one of several other words smart folks use.) At the end of the walkway he veered right, toward town, rather than steering left, up the hill toward his home.

Several weeks prior, Julian had learned of Main Street Cupcakes and their after-school special: a cup of hot cocoa and a cupcake. All for three dollars. A lot of kids from the school went there, and Julian hoped that if he went they might invite him to sit with them.

Plus, the cupcakes were really good.

He had gotten about halfway there when someone snuck up from behind.

"Greetings, Young Me!" Grown-up Julian said.

"*GAH!*" Julian yelled, jumping not quite out of his skin, but nearly out of his shoes. What are you doing here?" he asked.

"I could ask the same thing of you," Grown-up Julian said in a snooty tone of voice. "Shouldn't you be heading home? To check on me? To make sure I'm not getting into trouble?"

"I know how to stay out of trouble right now. So, I just assumed the future me would know how to as well."

"And yet here I am."

"Are you referring to this street? Or this decade?"

"Heh-heh. That's pretty funny, Young Me. Listen. You have a good sense of humor. In our family, it's a necessity—what the smart folks call a 'prerequisite.' Use it. Keep being funny. It's something that will come to define you. It will become your 'thing.' One of several, actually. But your sense of humor will be the main thing the other kids come to like about you."

"The main thing? You mean there are actually multiple things about me kids will like?"

"More than you know. But to say any more would risk—"

"Polluting the natural timeline. Got it. I *so* got it, get it? But, thanks. For the encouragement. Getting back to my original question, what are you doing here?"

"Guess what I figured out!" Grown-up Julian's excited tone gave Young Julian hope their problems would soon be over, ignoring for now the locked-away—what the smart folks call "confiscated"—eTab.

"What Cucumium is?"

"No. No luck there. Zero. Zip. Zilch. *Nada.* That's Spanish. But I did figure out that if I can tell you the winning lottery numbers for tonight, you'll never work a day in your life."

"Not now!"

"Later?"

"Maybe."

"*Yes!*" Grown-up Julian said, pumping his fist "We are going to be so rich!"

"So really, Grown-up Me, what are you doing here?"

"I got tired of sitting in our...your room." He laughed a little. "You know, it really isn't my room anymore. I mean, when I come home during breaks, I stay there. I sleep in the same bed. The *top bunk*," he added emphatically. "But it's not really my space anymore. And it used to seem so big to me. Now, not so much. I could say the same thing about Whispering Falls. Even though it's a small town, when we first moved here I remember thinking it was so big. I suppose that's because this is the first place we ever lived where I had the freedom to *go*. To be on my own. I was old enough, and I guess Mom and Dad thought it was safe enough."

Just outside downtown Grown-up Julian stopped, conveniently—what the smart folks call "serendipitously"—beneath the sign for Gronkowski's Groceries & Greetings, where Mr. and/or Mrs. Gronkowski always managed to greet the customers.

"Do you remember the first time Mom said, 'Julian, could you run to the supermarket for me?'" Grown-up Julian continued. "Of course you do. I still remember it. I remember feeling excited and terrified, all at the same time. I knew how to find the store and acted like I totally knew the way. 'Mom! Please! I go out the driveway, and down Washington, then turn right by the bank.' I was so casual about it. But when I actually did it, it felt like miles."

"And sometimes it still feels like I'm running through a maze now. Which is why you shouldn't be wandering around. You might get lost," Young Julian said.

"What are you talking about? I know this town better than you do. I know places you won't discover until...high school in some cases."

"Like what?" Julian said excitedly.

"Can't. Timeline, remember?"

"Sure. You're more than happy to spoil the secrets *you* want me to know. But when I ask a question, you clam up like a...clam," said Young Julian, dejected—what the cool folks call "bummed."

"OK, so the future you is fickle, too. Hey, do you think you can spot me three bucks?" Grown-up Julian asked.

"What for?"

"The cocoa and cupcake. Duh."

"How did you know about—Never mind."

Young Julian frowned.

"What's wrong?"

"It's like you know everything about me."

"I'll repeat myself. Duh. The bottom line is, if you know it, I know it. Or at least I knew it at one time. Though I do have a good memory. We get that from Mom, in case you hadn't noticed."

"She doesn't forget anything."

"No, she does not. Keep that in mind when you try to lie your way out of gluing Dylan to the wall by saying you were nowhere near the garage. She'll retrace your steps for you with pinpoint—what I call 'scary'—accuracy."

"Hey! No polluting!"

"Sorry. Forewarned is forearmed. But if you belay that one ill-advised prank, you won't get grounded and miss out on your first school dance and, by extension, your first slow dance."

"My first—"

"What do you know, there it is."

They reached the town square—in reality a triangle bounded by Washington, Main, and North Franklin Streets—turned right on Main, and headed past Whispering Falls S&L (which Julian assumed stood for Savings & Lollipops, since they always gave the latter out), Fallgreen's Drugstore, and Mr. Wiggles Slinky Shoppe. After dutifully looking both ways they crossed Main, pausing in the center of the triangle. Grown-up Julian looked appreciatively at the row of century-old two-story brick buildings lining North Franklin. Their flat roofs. Their arched second-floor windows. Their colorful awnings.

"What? What's wrong?" Young Julian asked.

"Nothing is wrong. Just take a look at the buildings. Each the same, yet at the same time, different. As a child, I barely noticed the architecture. But now I'm enjoying just standing and looking at it.

"It's good to be home, Young Me. When you're away at college, never pass up an opportunity to come back, even if it's just for a day. Promise?"

"Promise."

"Let's go. I'm buying."

"I thought you said you needed to borrow three dollars. I thought you didn't have any money."

"I was just fooling with you. The truth is, I already did borrow a few dollars." Grown-up Julian lowered his voice. "From Dad's wallet."

"Really?"

"Yup. Dad never pays attention to things like money, or matching socks. But, word of advice, don't go dipping from that well too often. Promise again?"

"Promise again. And I assume I should never dip from Mom's well?"

"Only if you want her to tell you how many bills are missing, and their serial numbers, before demanding that you empty your pockets, where she will then find them."

"Voice of experience?"

"No comment."

They continued their quest, completing the last leg by crossing over to North Franklin Street which, Julian realized for the first time, made Main Street Cupcakes an ironic name—what the smart folks call "moniker."

The Julians ordered the same thing, not surprisingly. Dark chocolate hot cocoa. No whipped cream (so the cup could be filled to the top with the delicious dark brew). And the Double Down, Double Trouble, Double Chocolate-Chip Cupcake. They took a table near the front, turned their chairs slightly, and leaned back against the rough, but cool, brick wall.

"I have so many good memories of this place," Grown-up Julian said.

"You do? We do? What kinds of good memories?" Young Julian asked.

"Why are you here?"

"Because these cupcakes *rock!*"

"They do. But you could get one to go. So why are you *here?*"

Young Julian knew he could not lie to his older self.

"Because other kids are."

"Indeed they are. And in due time, you will be sitting with someone other than your future self. At least, I hope I won't be back."

"You're sure? You're really sure about this whole making friends thing."

"I think I was there for it. So, yeah, really sure."

"Who? Who will I become friends with?"

"Well, let me think."

At that moment a floorboard squeaked, which floorboards that have been trod upon for a hundred years or so are inclined do.

"Stand up!" Grown-up Julian commanded. "Stand up and get ready to catch."

"What? Why?"

"Don't argue. Just...Sheesh!"

Grown-up Julian, much stronger than his younger self, grabbed ninety-two-pound Young Julian, brought him to his feet, wheeled him around, and extended his arms just as a boy fell into them. Young Julian's natural reflexes, sharpened from years of dodging his dad's misfires, helped him keep the boy and his hot chocolate-cupcake combo upright and off the floor.

"Great catch, Julian," Grown-up Julian said.

"Yeah, thanks," said the boy.

"You're welcome," said Young Julian, sort of recognizing him. "Say, aren't you in my grade?"

"I think so. My name is Tim. Tim Towers. I'm in Mr. Santayana's class."

"Yeah, I go to him for history. I'm in Mrs. Stern's class."

"I thought so. I thought I've seen you in the halls. You're new this year, right?"

"Right."

The boys stood in silence, unsure of what to do next.

Grown-up Julian spoke. "Well, maybe you two wild guys will see each other in here again sometime."

"Maybe," they said, together.

"Nice meeting you," they said, again, together.

Tim took his still-intact after-school snack and found an empty table near the back of the store.

"Well, that was a productive two minutes," Grown-up Julian said, plopping himself down, Young Julian following suit. Or seat, as it were.

"I have to ask. How did you know?"

"That's a broad question."

"How did you know to stand me up and make me do the arm thing?"

"Simple. Because I remembered. I heard the floor-board creak, and it triggered a memory of this day. This day, eight years ago, from my perspective. Today, from yours."

"Wow. You're amazing."

"You too, Young Me. Actually, you did a better job. I let a few drops of his cocoa spill."

"Still, the fact that your brain still works at such an advanced age speaks to...I don't know. Genetics, or maybe the proper lifestyle choices I will make."

Young Julian had no clue that *no* 20-year-old saw himself as "advanced" in age. As such, the clipped tone painting "Advanced" Julian's voice went over his head.

"Thanks, *Young* Me. Apparently they still haven't fixed that loose floorboard."

"What do you mean, *still?*"

"It's been loose forever."

"Yeah, but if you remember it being loose this day—and obviously you did remember it—then it couldn't be fixed. At least not yet."

"Oh yeah. Wow. This is getting more and more complicated."

"And now I get to say, DUH!"

"You got me, Funny Guy."

"Yeah, I'm a funny guy. It will be my 'thing.' I just can't wait until that whole kids liking me thing you talked about happens. Any day now would be fine."

"Well, you can start tomorrow by sitting back there when you come in," Grown-up Julian said.

"Why?"

"Because that's where he likes to sit. He's kind of shy."

"Who?"

"Your first best friend, that's who."

"Him?"

"Yup. Timmy Towers will be your first best friend. Kind of sad, when you think about it. You didn't have a best friend until age twelve."

"We moved a lot. Remember?"

"Yes, I remember. Still, you could have done more to make friends at the other schools."

"You could have, too."

"Touché."

"He's kind of small."

"Who?"

"That Tim guy."

"Heh-heh. Just you wait. In a year or two 'that Tim guy' will have a growth spurt. In fact, they'll become an annual occurrence. He'll play center for the basketball team and be Mr. Popular. He'll be a good friend to have."

"Him?"

Grown-up Julian simply nodded.

"If you insist."

"You're not convinced. Look, I totally understand what you're going through. Literally, I do. I did. Thinking you don't belong. What the smart folks call being 'ostracized.' Feeling like an oddball—what the smart folks call an 'outcast.'"

"Even though I always appreciate learning new words, you really don't need to teach me every synonym for loser."

"The point, Young Me, is that all kids your age feel that way. Heck, most grown-ups do."

"Really?"

"Really. The trick is just learning to overcome it. Or just hiding it. But believe me when I tell you, even when you're...me, there will be situations which bring you right back here. To the insecurity and self-doubt of age twelve."

"Great," Young Julian said in a tone that indicated he found the news to be anything but. The two

Julians took simultaneous final swigs from the mugs monogrammed with MSC. "Well, on that happy note."

"Shall we, Young Me?"

"Yeah, let's go. So, you really, truly, cross-your-heart promise everything will turn out fine? That I won't spend the rest of my life as an outcast? That I'll be—"

In addition to the family dinner table rules, another basic tenet of good manners Mrs. Newcomber insisted upon was to always look at someone as you are speaking to him or her. So ingrained was her mandate that Julian had not yet come to terms with the idea of suspending the practice when performing a challenging simultaneous task, such as flying an airplane or walking. As such, the inwardly swinging door barely missed him. But the soft voice certainly connected.

"Hi, Julian."

"Oh, hi. You're..."

"I'm Lisa. I sit in front of you."

"I know. You pass papers back to me. Then I hand them up to you. You write left handed. You swing your feet a lot. And you twist your hair around your finger when you're thinking," he said, immediately fearing he had crossed the line between noticing her quirks and cataloging them.

Grown-up Julian, who had been watching the conversation cleared his throat.

"Say, Julian. Aren't you going to introduce me to this *very nice* young lady?"

"Sorry. Lisa, this is—"

"Brad," Grown-up Julian said, breaking in—what the smart folks call "interjecting."

"Brad. He's my—"

"Older cousin."

"Older cousin."

"So you sit in front of Julian? In Mrs. Stern's class?"

"Yes," she said.

"She teaches math, doesn't she?"

"Yes."

Now came Young Julian's turn to watch the exchange and wonder when he might be able to get back into it.

"You really rock in that class, don't you, Julian?"

"Sort of...Kind of...I guess so," said Young Julian.

"Math is your best subject, isn't it?"

"Sort of...Kind of...I guess so."

"Really?" Lisa asked. "Because I'm having trouble with it."

"Then you need a friend like Julian here. Maybe some time he could—"

"—help you study," Young Julian said, regaining some measure of control over the conversation.

"I'd like that," Lisa said.

"Great," Young Julian said.

"Yeah, great," Grown-up Julian said.

"Well, I'd better get in line before they're all sold out. The best cupcakes tend to go quickly after school lets out. Are you leaving?"

"Yeah. We had ours. And we need to get home."

"Oh. OK. It was good seeing you, Julian," she said,

stepping into the queue and casting a quick glance back in his direction.

"Same here," he said, waving, then sighing audibly, puppy-dog eyes following her every move.

"What was that, Young Me?" Grown-up Julian asked, his tone more than a touch cloying.

"Nothing."

"Say it."

"OK. She is cute. A little. Maybe"

"And was it just me, or did she seem disappointed to hear you needed to leave?"

Young Julian didn't know where to go with *that* and quickly changed the subject. "Oh, and *Brad?*"

"It's as good a name as any. After all, what guy doesn't want to be Brad Pitt?"

"Who?"

"He's an actor."

"Never heard of him."

"He's the voice of Metro Man."

"Oh. Him."

"Let's get out of here. I'm sure we have work to do. At the very least, you have homework to do," Grown-up (and responsible) Julian said.

"When did you become Mom?"

"When I got smart."

"I suppose there's an insult in there somewhere."

"Young Me, Young Me, let us not dwell on petty putdowns. We should instead revel in the successes of this glorious afternoon. We, no, *you* earned friendship points with Timmy Towers and Lisa Honeywell. Could this day get any better?"

Young Julian hated to pop this bubble of joy. But sooner or later he would have to.

"Well…"

CHAPTER 10

"It's Pickle hunting season!"

The mighty and warm wind from the south—what the smart folks call a "sirocco"—carrying the unmistakable scent of bacon saved Young Julian from having to explain his "well…"

For now.

"Oh no," the two Julians said in unison.

"Ugh! Biff Masterson." Grown-up Julian added. "I forgot that was today."

"At least this means you managed to live through it."

"Yeah, I suppose I did," Grown-up Julian said. "Pickle hunting? I never did understand that one. It's not like you need to hunt them. They come in a jar. And even if they didn't, I'm not sure you really can 'hunt' a vegetable. Or any inert object, for that matter."

Biff snorted and acted like—what the smart folks call "pantomimed"—a bull about to charge, scraping a foot backward along the sidewalk and stripping off several inches of concrete in the process.

"I'm so not in the mood for a wedgie or a swirlie or a wringie," Young Julian said.

"Oh yeah. I remember that, too. I wouldn't have thought it possible for one person to pick up another and twist him like a dishrag. Don't worry, Young Me. You're not getting Biffed. Not today. Not on my watch."

"What do we do?"

"Follow me," Grown-up Julian said, leading Young Julian up North Franklin and away from the Biffdozer.

Biff remained on the other side of Washington Street, about 100 feet away, waiting for the Red Hand to give way to the Walking Guy, whose white luminescence would bless his passage across the busy intersection. Once given the (literal) green light, he pulled an imaginary chain above his head, threw open his mouth, and emitted a perfect-sounding air horn noise.

The sonic calling card inspired the Julians to double their pace. Occupying a prime spot just past the point where North Franklin met Main—the hypotenuse of the Town Triangle—was the Fireside Book Shop. More to the point, it sat just past a slight bend in the sidewalk, meaning Biff did not have a straight line of vision as they entered.

"In here," Grown-up Julian said, opening the door as the little bell above cheerfully announced their arrival. He steered them right, then left, maneuvering between the biographies and new arrivals as he headed toward the rear of the store.

"We'll be trapped!" Young Julian said, fear creeping into his voice. Indeed, just as they entered the back room the bell sang out again, though this time it sounded more like a funeral processional. The door slammed. After a moment of merciful silence, the floor creaked under duress.

"No worries," Grown-up Julian said, whispering nonetheless.

"Sure. You don't have any. But I've got enough for both of us. You may not have noticed this, but you're a grown-up. He's not going to touch you. But me..."

"He won't touch either."

"And you know this because..."

"Because I know two things you don't."

"What? Jujitsu and levitation?"

"No. Well, maybe. I can't say. It's complicated."

"Then...?"

"One, Biff is allergic to books. Literally."

"You can't be seri—"

A gale-force wind coursed through the store. On its heels came a titanic ACHOC!

"That ought to keep him occupied. Or should I say allergized?"

"Great. He's sneezing. You do understand he's physically capable of blocking both aisles between here and the front of the store."

"And, drum roll, please. Thing I know number two. There's a back door."

"There is?"

Grown-up Julian extended his arm in a way that said, "After you."

Indeed, around the shelf labeled Misprints & Misfits lay salvation.

Without a bell.

Safely outside, Young Julian breathed a sigh of relief.

"How did you know?"

"About what?"

"Both."

"Well, once Biff chased me into the intermediate school library. That's how I learned about his aversion to literary diversion."

"It's going to take me a few minutes to figure out that last sentence. In the meantime, what's the other?"

"The better question is, how did you *not* know? Haven't you ever been in there?"

"No. We've only been here a few months, remember?"

"Fair enough. Trust me. In a few years you'll know the place inside and out. It's where you're going to get your first job."

"I will? Doing what?"

"Just stuff like stocking shelves, calling customers to say their order is in, and occasionally fumigating the place to kill the bookworms. Just kidding about that last one. Mr. Lewis, the owner, is a good man. He'll treat you well."

"Sounds good, I suppose. But a bookstore?"

"Yeah. What's wrong with a *bookstore?*" Grown-up Julian perfectly imitated what Mrs. Newcomber often called Julian's "my life is *soooo* horrible tone of voice." Which was not surprising.

"Bookstores are boring."

"Maybe some are. But this is a magical place."

"Magic as in Houdini, or magic as in Peter Pan?"

"I mean, books are magic. What else can deliver you to exotic lands, other planets, or even other times? What else can do that? I mean, assuming you don't have an enhanced eTab and an adventurous stupidity streak." Grown-up Julian said, sounding once again like their mom. "That's all I meant."

"Yeah, that's what Mom says. *Always*," Young Julian said in the "my life is *soooo* horrible tone of voice."

"Let's get home, Young Me. We'll take the stealth route."

A muffled explosion from within Fireside told them Biff remained at war with his nose.

"I think I might have found his kryptonite," Young Julian said.

"Come to think of it, maybe that's the reason we started working there."

Walking back toward Washington by slinking through the parking lot behind the shops on North Franklin, Young Julian noticed a small sign affixed to a weathered wall.

"The Paris Room? *PARIS!?*"

"Chill. It's a bar. Or, a bistro, as you can see," he said, pointing to the sign above the door.

"Oh."

"What?" asked Grown-up Julian.

"Nothing. It's just that for a minute I thought maybe…"

Had Grown-up Julian been mid-sip on any drink, he would have done a spit-take. As it was, he executed the empty-mouth equivalent.

"Pffft! That the Paris Room would somehow transport you to Paris?"

Young Julian looked down and kicked the gravel a little. Grown-up Julian laughed heartily, occasionally crossing over into guffawing, augmented by emphatic knee-slapping

"Well," Young Julian said defensively, "given everything that's happened in the past twenty-four hours, it didn't seem outside the realm of possibility."

Grown-up Julian quieted down.

"I suppose you have a point," he conceded. "But no. It's a place to dine and wine, the latter only if you're a grown-up. No teleportation service here, Young Me."

"Too bad. It would be cool. If this place could magically send you to Paris. I'd love to go there."

"You will. Senior year." Young Julian perked up. "It's kind of a funny story, actually. Mom was out of town for the World Semaphore Championships."

"She's always said she wanted to do that."

"Yes. So, Dad had to take care of everything. The cooking went OK. But when it came to reading and answering any correspondence from the school…"

"I know this won't end well," Young Julian said.

"One of the emails was from the Whispering Falls Club *Français*, announcing the annual France trip. But

Dad was tinkering with his glasses at the time. Trying to add an electron microscope to them, or something like that. Turns out, he thought he read 'French dip,' his favorite kind of sandwich. He signed me up, apparently not questioning why a lunch entrée would cost four thousand dollars. By the time he realized his mistake—which is to say, by the time Mom saw the credit card bill and flipped out—it was too late to back out. Three months later, I'm on a plane to Paris."

"Cool! When do I start studying French?"

"You don't."

"I don't?"

"Nope. We stick with good old *Español*."

"You mean I will actually...?"

"Spend a month in France without speaking a word of the language? Yup."

"Should I be afraid?"

"We managed. We always do. You're just going to have to trust me on that one."

Young Julian nodded in overt agreement, but covertly wondered whether everything really would be as easy as his future self claimed.

"Speaking of trust," Young Julian began, "didn't we have an agreement? No revealing the future unless it's life or death. Working at the bookstore and flying off to Paris"

"Is technically about life. So, I'm safe. Now let's get home, Young Me. We've got a power supply problem to solve."

By the time they'd put the business district behind them, Young Julian had done likewise with the dire news he dreaded sharing with Grown-up Julian when they'd left the cupcake shop. Grown-up Julian had not.

"About that 'Well...' Well what?" he asked.

"What?"

"A few minutes ago, I said something about this day getting better. And you said, 'Well...' with a distinct tone of hesitation in your voice. Remember?"

"Oh, that. It's...nothing," Young Julian said, trying to minimize—what the smart folks call "downplay"—the bombshell to come.

"You're doing it again."

"I am?"

"Spill it. What happened?"

"Well, maybe we have a problem."

"We do?"

"Sort of. Do you remember Mr. Nitro?"

"Remember him? He was my favorite teacher. He changed my life. Do you want to know why?"

"Does it have anything to do with returning the eTab he took because I was using it in class?"

"No. Nothing to do with that. It's because he—Wait. Did you say he took the eTab?" Grown-up Julian asked.

"Yes."

"Because you were using it in class?"

"Yes."

"Why would you do that?"

"Because he was talking about copper. And the symbol for copper is Cu. And Cu made me think of Cucumium. And then his voice stopped talking, even though his lips kept moving, and other voices started singing, and—"

"Oh, yeah. I remember having classes in that room. You know, to this day, when I need to study for a science test, I put on some choral music. Helps me focus."

"Got it. Choral music to study. Anyway, it's gone. Well, it's not gone. It's locked in his desk."

"So what's the problem? Work on a deep, sincere apology and the exact words you can use to ask—"

"But then he started sneezing and honking, and he ran out the door. I'm pretty sure he left. I heard something out in the parking lot that sounded like a jet engine."

"Oh yeah. The Lab-Ratmobile."

"Heh-heh. That's a good one."

"Thanks. You came up with it."

"I did? I don't remem—Oh, I get it."

Grown-up Julian thought for a minute. Young Julian could tell by the way his eyes and lips were moving without seeing or speaking. Then a look of worry flashed onto Grown-up Julian's face.

"He has the eTab! Oh, man! Could this day get any worse?"

Young Julian was somewhat surprised by his older self's reaction.

"At first, I thought the same thing. But maybe I was overreacting. I mean, it's locked in his desk. As you said, what's the problem? I should be able to get it tomorrow and—"

"Today is Thursday. Tomorrow is Friday. The day after that is Saturday."

"Are you sure?" Julian began counting on his fingers for comic—what his dad called "genetically-programmed wise guy"—effect.

"Am I sure?"

"Seriously? I think we learned the days of the week in preschool."

"The point is, if Mr. Nitro isn't there tomorrow, allergies and household HAZMAT events being two common reasons for him to call in sick or glowing, then your eTab will stay in his desk all weekend. And I don't know that we *will* need yours to send me back. But if we do..."

"But if we do, the problem is you don't have enough battery to make it through the weekend. And if it completely dies, the clock app will get erased, and you'll be stuck here on the *bottom bunk* forever."

"Yes. Except for the bottom bunk part. I thought we might—"

"Don't even go there." Young Julian barked, his pent-up anger finally boiling over. "You sure are creating a mess for me...us."

"Yeah, but not as bad as the mess that you'll create at the end of sixth grade. Yeah, I probably should also go back to then, and tell myself to not pull that stupid stunt."

"Well, you're here right now with yourself, in person. Since you've already made an exception—what the smart folks call 'set a precedent'—for sharing news that spares the family from harm, I suppose you could tell me what it is."

"OK. Don't break into the school on the night before your last day of sixth grade and spread around all the Evaporated Mouse Powder that Dad made. I mean, you couldn't know they'd polish the floors the next day, but whew! What a mess that was."

"Got it. I won't break into the school and—Wait! You said you broke into the school?"

"Yes."

"The intermediate school?"

"Yes."

"The school where I go now, and where my eTab is locked in a desk drawer?"

"Yes."

"Could we do it—break in—again?"

"Sure. But Dad hasn't invented the Evaporated Mouse Powder yet. So why would we—Oh, I get it."

"Grown-up Me, I think you and I are going to have an adventure—what the smart folks call an 'escapade'—tonight."

CHAPTER 11

That evening, the two Julians prepared for their mission. While Young Julian was downstairs eating with the family, Grown-up Julian was out back, in his dad's lab, acquiring some helpful supplies—what the smart folks call "accoutrements." Back up in the room, he laid out the spoils.

"Night vision goggles. Master-Key-In-A-Can. The Cloak Of Invisibility. Granola bars, in case we get hungry."

"Invisibility?" Young Julian said happily. "That will make this so much—"

"Just kidding. Come on. That's *Harry Potter*. But all kidding aside, *this* will come in handy," he said, holding out a really large tube of toothpaste.

"Wait. Didn't I just see that?"

"Probably at dinner some night. Dad called it No Squeak. He designed it to stop floors and doors and drawers from squeaking. But one time I got some on my shoes. And a little on my hands. And I found I could climb walls. Just like Spiderman. Isn't that great?"

"Yeah, if it were true."

"What do you mean?"

"*Star Trek. Harry Potter. Spiderman.* Any time you talk about something really cool, it's just a movie reference. You're not fooling me again."

"Oh no. This time I'm serious."

"Really?"

"Really. How do you think I got into the school to play that sixth-grade prank? The one I told you not to do." Grown-up Julian pointed skyward. "Up the wall, in the window. Oh, which reminds me. You probably want to bring another pair of shoes. Otherwise, you're going to have a dickens of a time trying to walk home with this stuff all over the bottom of the ones you used to climb the wall. And get some gloves. Unless you want your hands to stick to Mr. Nitro's desk drawer, and anything else you happen to touch."

"So how do we get it off?"

"After about a day it just evaporates. Or does this stuff explode?"

Young Julian's heart skipped a beat.

"No," Grown-up Julian said after thinking—what the smart folks call "mulling"—it over. "This evaporates. It doesn't explode. Probably. Are we ready?"

"In a minute. I think I need to go to the bathroom and get sick."

"Why? Nerves?"

"No. The spinach. The spinach you made me heap onto my plate. The spinach Mom made me eat some of, right in front of her. She claimed it was for Dylan's and Olivia's benefit. To show them it's OK. But I think she has it out for me. No matter the reason, it was *totally gross!*"

"You mean, totally *yes!*"

"When did I stop being me, and turn into you?"

"Every single day, Young Me. Every single day."

"I'm not sure I like it."

Young Julian and Grown-up Julian spent the next three hours honing their plan and reviewing the logistics. (Though, in reality, they spent most of the time testing different substances for suitability as invisible ink, and practicing hand signals for maneuvers like Move Forward and Run Away!) In the end, they came up with a seven-phase plan.

I. *GET THERE.*
2. *GET UP.*
3. *GET IN.*
4. *GET IT.*
5. *GET OUT.*
6. *GET DOWN.*
7. *GET HOME.*

They included an extra step—what the smart folks call an "addendum" or a "codicil."

8. *GET AWAY WITH IT.*

After the sane members of the family had gone to bed—and Mr. Newcomber was in his lab, where he often fell asleep, usually to wake up with his face chemically bonded to his workbench—Young Julian and Grown-up Julian crept down the stairs and out the back door. Though they probably didn't have to, they hugged the shadows and ducked behind trees whenever a car or suspicious squirrel approached, like the cool secret operative agents they were.

As they snuck up the walkway to the front of the school, Young Julian was struck by just how deserted it was. It felt, to him, even lonelier than when filled with kids, if that was possible.

Too soon for his liking, Young Julian found himself standing beneath Mr. Nitro's window, staring at his goal, three stories up.

"Why couldn't this be like the elementary school? One floor."

"What the smart folks call a 'story' and the British folks call a 'storey,'" added Grown-up Julian. "Get your gloves on and stand close to the building."

Grown-up Julian unscrewed the cap.

"Now, just a bit," he said. "Maybe a quarter-sized amount. Smear it on the toes of your shoes, not the bottoms. Otherwise, you'll have to take them off when you get up there."

Young Julian applied a small amount to each.

"It smells nice. Like kiwifruit."

"Dad's favorite fruit. By the way, someday, when he offers you his special deodorant that smells like kiwifruit, say no. It attracts yellow jackets. And hummingbirds."

"Got it," he said as he rubbed some of the goo on the palms of his gloves. "I think I'm set."

"Good luck," Grown-up Julian said. "See you on the ground. That's what the guys who stay back at the airfield—nice and safe and warm—say to the guys who actually fly the planes on the dangerous missions, the stare-in-the-face-of-doom-and-laugh guys. Ha-Ha! Seriously, don't fall."

"Thanks, I—Wait! Aren't you coming?"

"No."

"Why not?"

"Two reasons. One, I only brought one pair of shoes from the future. Though, technically, from the past. The point is, I can't slop up these ones with No Squeak."

"We could have grabbed a pair of Dad's shoes. Your feet look about the same size as his."

"True, but..." His pause gave Young Julian pause. "More to the point, if things go wrong, I've got to leave you. *I* can't get caught in there. It might be a little tough to explain."

"I suppose you're right."

"I wish I weren't. But you'll be fine."

Young Julian nodded, and put a cautious—what the smart folks call "tentative"—hand on the wall. Then another, up a little higher. One foot. Both feet. He reached, reached, pulled, pulled, stepped, stepped. Suddenly, he *was* Spiderman.

"Wow," he said from his new vantage point ten feet up.

"I know!"

Young Julian zipped swiftly up the rough brick and reached the ledge in no time flat. The window was open. He knew it would be. It was always open. Rumor had it that the one (and only) time Mr. Nitro did close the window before leaving for the night, the accumulation of fumes and aethers had formed some kind of super-fertilizer that descended on the terrarium in the corner; he arrived the next day to find moss and clinging vines had overtaken the class-room. After that, Mr. Ajax, the janitor, told him to *never* close the window. (On the bright side, if it were not for the little vegetative mishap, Mr. Ajax would not have his pet monkey.)

"This is going to work. This is going to work," Julian said as he prepared to (in theory) commit his first felony.

He took one step and...

WOOP-WOOP-WOOP-WOOP-WOOP!

Young Julian stuck his head out the window and yelled down.

"I don't remember you saying anything about alarms!"

"They weren't any."

"How could there not be?"

"I don't know, I...Come to think of it, when I pulled my stunt it was during the Great Spring Blackout. That sure was one of Dad's better ones. I remember hearing reports of power outages as far away as To-ledo, and—"

"What do I do?"

"My number one suggestion would be HURRY UP!"

Young Julian ran—as fast as one can run with

wall-climbing goo on his shoes—over to the desk. He checked first to see if it would just open. No luck.

Woop-woop-woop-woop-woop!

He realized for the first time he probably should have read and memorized the directions on the label of the Master-Key-In-A-Can *before* this little stunt.

"Let's see. 'Shake well for seventeen seconds.' *Seventeen!*" He shook the can for the longest seventeen seconds of his life.

Woop-woop-woop-woop-woop!

"Come on!" Grown-up Julian shouted.

"Next, 'Place tube into spray nozzle. Place other end of tube into lock. Press down on spray nozzle for one thousand one.' Pressing. Counting. One thousand one. 'Stop. Wait for one thousand two.' One thousand one, one thousand two."

Woop-woop-woop-woop-woop!

"And finally, 'Turn.' Turning."

The lock opened. (To be honest, Young Julian was somewhat surprised.) The eTab was there. He stuffed it in his backpack. Despite his rising (increasing?) panic, he had the good sense—what the smart folks call "insight"—to close the drawer, relock it, and pack away the Master-Key-In-A-Can before racing back to the window.

"Come on! I hear sirens," Grown-up Julian called up.

Young Julian clambered down squirrel-style and hit the ground crawling, before evolving to walking, then to running. In a blur they no longer were crime scene fixtures, but rather, two regular, ordinary, average citizens out for a late-evening, curfew-violating, totally not suspicious mad dash up the sidewalk. Five minutes later, the perpetrators—what the police folks call "perps"—were back in their room, congratulating each other on a job well done, listening to the growing chorus of sirens down in town, centered somewhere around...the intermediate school, perhaps.

"I can't believe we pulled that off," Young Julian said.

"You know, thinking about it now—what the smart folks call 'in hindsight'—I guess I should have also grabbed the can of Alarm-B-Gone from Dad's workbench."

"You think?"

"Next time."

"There won't be a next time."

"No comment."

"Fine. I probably don't want to know anyway."

"Seriously, Young Me, that was a great job. Nerves of steel. Resolve of iron. Appendix of aluminum.

"Appendix of aluminum?"

"I guess I ran out of metaphorical steam. Regardless, this calls for a celebration. After all, you didn't get arrested. And you didn't fall and break your neck which, thinking it over now, would have seriously impacted my future. All in all, I'd call it a good mission."

"So how does Future Me celebrate?"

"With chocolate milk and chocolate-chip cookies." The final word, Grown-up Julian said with a melodic flourish.

"That sounds great. But we don't have any cookies in the house."

"We don't?" Grown-up Julian said, arching an eyebrow.

"No. We never do. Mom says they're bad for us. So she gives us treats like asparagus-kelp crackers. Bleh."

"Heh-heh."

"What?" Young Julian said.

"No cookies? Anywhere in the house? Yeah, that's what Mom *tells* you."

"It's not the truth?"

"Not even close. Not even within the sphere of sort-of truths."

"Cookies? Here? In this house? Where are they?!" Julian said, reining in his "playground voice" as best as he could.

"That's funny. Your voice whispered it. But your brain was *yelling* it. Follow me, Young Me."

Down in the kitchen, Grown-up Julian switched on the small light above the stove.

"I have to tell you, Grown-up Me, a year ago I would have said you were fibbing, or half-truthing, or something. But just the other night, after Mom thought I'd gone to bed, I came down here and surprised her. When she saw me, she put her hand over her mouth, then chewed and swallowed quickly. She asked me what I was doing and seemed kind of guilty. I could have sworn I smelled chocolate on her breath. So, I figured she was hiding something. Something good. Something forbidden."

"What the German folks call *'verboten.'*"

"Whatever. The next day, I searched every cabinet and cupboard in here. There wasn't even a single crumb of a cookie. And why am I still telling you these things? You already know all my stories."

"Indeed I do. But you tell them so well. Now," Grown-up Julian said, rubbing his hands together, "observe."

He walked over to the sink.

"See this?" He said pointing to the hot water tap.

"You mean the hot water tap that doesn't work? That never worked?"

"Did you ever stop to think about it? Does Dad *ever* let something go un-fixed?"

"I guess not. I just figured he came up with some far-out invention to boil water and he didn't care if it worked or not."

"Oh, it works all right. Just not how you think."

Grown-up Julian pulled the spigot up. At first, nothing happened, reinforcing Young Julian's skepticism. But before he could deliver a sarcastic riposte like "Uh-huh," the floor began trembling. Just a bit, a slight hum preceding a faint metallic grind. With a hiss, the refrigerator slid to one side, revealing a secret pantry stocked with goodies—what Mrs. Newcomber called "contraband."

"Ta-da! What the French folks call *'Voilà!'*"

"OMG. How did you find this?"

"You have to pay attention to *everything* around this house, Young Me. Though, now I may have created what is known as a 'temporal feedback loop.' Or something like that." He stared off into space, like his dad, as he began thinking out loud. "So I, at age twenty, show it to myself, at age twelve. Now, the twelve-year-old me knows about it. So, when I'm twenty, I'll be able to return to this time and show it to—"

"Get out of my way," Young Julian said, trying to push past his older counterpart.

"Not so fast," said the older, wiser version, throwing out an arm to block Young Julian's assault on the assortment of sugary snacks. He pinched a small quantity of flour from the jar on the counter and poured it into his cupped hand. Standing before the portal to temptation, he blew the powder into the opening. Four red laser beams cut through the floating dust.

"Whoa!" said Young Julian.

"I know. And it triggers a *silent* alarm. Took me months to figure that one out. I thought Mom was just in her hear-all, know-all mode."

He gingerly reached between the still-glowing photonic tripwires, selected a bag emblazoned with a photograph of a huge cookie, and carefully pulled it out.

Five minutes later, the Julians were reveling in the glory of their accomplishment, and basking in the illicit delicity of the cookies.

"These are *so good!*"

"I know. Quadruple Choco Chewy Delights. They're Dad's favorite. Mom, in contrast, prefers standard chocolate-chip cookies."

"Yes, I can see how one might overload on the sheer volume of chocolate in these things."

"What do you think fuels Dad?"

"I just assumed it was natural."

"Technically accurate, since chocolate is derived from cocoa beans, which are a naturally occurring substance."

"I like how we think."

"What a night. Contraband cookies. And a perfectly—what the smart folks call 'flawlessly'—executed mission."

"I just thought of something," Young Julian said. "What happens when Mr. Nitro decides to give me back the eTab, and finds out it's not there?"

"Just tell him he already gave it back."

"That won't work."

"Sure it will. Why do you think he keeps his car keys and his lunch box attached to his belt with a chain? Because he's so absent-minded, if he set them down anywhere, he'd forget where he put them. I've heard rumors he has a sign on the inside of his front door: Look Down! Make Sure You're Wearing Pants!"

Young Julian was grateful he had swallowed the swig of milk two seconds earlier. He was also just grateful, period.

"I couldn't have done this without you," Young Julian said.

"An oxymoron, if I ever heard one. Or was it a palindrome? I can never keep the two words straight."

"No, I really mean that. You've got guts. You traveled back to the Civil War. You planned a break-in at the school. More than once, from what you've said. But that means I went back to the Civil War. And I planned a break-in at the school. I can't do those things. So, how could you?"

"Why do you say you can't do those things?"

"Because I don't have the guts," Young Julian said quietly.

"Then you're saying I really don't have the guts," Grown-up Julian said.

"But that's not possible."

"Quite the puzzle—what the smart folks call a 'conundrum.' Isn't it?"

"I wonder what went wrong...or right."

"You know, I said I missed a few classes where we talked about this time travel stuff. But, earlier I mentioned temporal feedback—"

Grown-up Julian froze. From upstairs came a faint *jingle jingle jingle*.

"Oh man!" Grown-up Julian said.

"What is that?"

"It's Dad!"

"How do you know?"

"Do you remember Dad saying something to Mom about putting bells on his shoes? Sometime? Ever?"

"Yeah. Last night at dinner."

"Well, listen."

The jingle grew more manic. A shadow loomed outside the kitchen.

"Oops."

"Dive! Dive!" Grown-up Julian grabbed his glass and plate, and dove beneath the table.

Scant seconds later, Mr. Newcomber strode in. The lines on his left cheek matched—what the smart folks call "corresponded with"—the slats of wood from the surface of his workbench.

"Hey, Son Number One. Or should that be Number One Son? I'll have to ask your mother. She always was the literate one."

"Hi, Dad."

"Oho! I see you found the secret cookie stash."

"I'm afraid so."

"How long have you known about it?"

"Not long." Julian's younger, more sensitive ears heard his older, and allegedly more mature, self snickering beneath the table. A quick kick shut him up.

"My first bit of advice is to not tell your mother you know about it," Mr. Newomber said, sliding silently into his chair, nearly kicking Grown-up Julian's head in the process. Otherwise she'll move it. Or better said, she'll make me move it. My second bit of advice is to not tell your mother I told you that. Otherwise I'll have to move something else. Like your bedroom, to the roof."

"Deal."

"What are you doing up at this hour of the night?"

"I just couldn't sleep. I had a busy day."

Julian went to scratch his head but stopped when he realized he could not put the glass down. Apparently, some of the No Squeak had leaked through one of the gloves and waited deviously for the perfect opportunity to bond to something. He tried to act naturally. At least as naturally as one can act with a glass of milk glued to one's hand. Mr. Newcomber chuckled a little.

"What's so funny? And why are you looking at me like that, Dad? Because it may *look* like this glass is attached—"

Mr. Newcomber waved his hand a little.

"It's funny. Seeing you down here and having this conversation with you. It just makes me think of when I used to sit at the kitchen table with my Dad, have a snack, and discuss things. And now here I am, all grown up—your mother's opinion notwithstanding—doing the same thing with my son. And someday you'll be grown up, and so on, and so on, and so on."

"Whoa, Dad. Let's get me out of high school first. For that matter, let's get me into high school."

"Trust me. Before you know it, you'll be escaping from intermediate school."

"I hear that."

"And then high school. Then college. You know, when you have a baby, folks always say 'Remember these years. They go by so quickly.' Those folks were right. I still see you as the little boy I used to give baths to and tuck in every night after a spirited reading of *Goodnight Moon*. But if I close my eyes, I can almost envision the man you'll be in ten years, or even when you're my age."

The off-the-cuff remark hit too close to home. And this time, Julian's timing with regard to the mouthful of milk proved less than ideal.

"Napkin?"

"Thanks," Julian said, cleaning up the aftermath of his spit-take with his free hand. "So what do you think I will look like in one hundred years, Dad?"

"Taller, I hope."

The fact his dad ignored the dig—what kids in Julian's school call a "burn"—meant he didn't really hear Julian's question. But his eyes had that faraway look—what Julian's mom called "Dad being Dad."

"So, am I going to be just like you?"

"Oh, heavens! I hope not."

"Really?" The answer truly surprised Julian.

"No, no. I don't want you to be just like me."

"Why not?"

"I'd like to think I'm a pretty decent guy. And a pretty good father. But I'm not perfect. Nobody is. I have my flaws. I've made my mistakes. Lord knows I've spent too many years of my life regrowing my eyebrows. And I know I tend to drive your mother crazy." Mr. Newcomber lowered his voice and leaned in, even though he and Julian—the Julians, actually—were the only people in the room. "Though it's often a *very* short drive," he whispered. "And if you ever tell your mother I said anything even remotely like that I will deny it up and down—what the smart folks call 'vehemently.' And then move your bedroom to the roof."

"Your secret's safe with me, Dad."

"The thing is, your mother and I work well together. In areas where I'm weak, she's strong. And vice versa. That's what you look for in a husband or wife.

Someone who fills in the pieces you're missing. So no, I don't want you to be just like me. I want you to be yourself and try to incorporate the best pieces of Mom and me."

"So, Mom is weak in some areas?"

"Did I actually *say* that?"

"You suggested—what the smart folks call 'implied'—it"

"I've taught you well, Number One Son... or Son Number One..."

"So exactly what pieces is Mom missing?"

"A very good question. A question best answered some other day and some other time," Mr. Newcomber said, getting up from the table. "Speaking of another time, I think it's time for me to go to bed. And I *know* it's time for you to go to bed. Good night, Julian," he said, leaning over and kissing his son on the top of the head. He laughed a little. "In three years or so, you so won't want me doing that. It's normal— what the golfing folks call 'par for the course.' But it will still make me sad." He jingled out of the room and up the stairs before Julian had a chance to say, "Never, Dad."

Grown-up Julian waited until the sound of bells was gone before coming out of his hiding place.

"He's right, you know."

"About what?"

"Pretty much all of it. But I was thinking of the part about how you won't want him kissing you good night in a few years. Or even hugging you."

"I can't believe that."

But Young Julian saw in his future self a look that said it was true and that he would regret it. He wanted to talk about it, but quickly decided it was something he'd rather not know.

"So did Mom put bells on all of Dad's shoes?"

"Pretty much. Except for his running shoes. That would have been embarrassing and obnoxious."

"Agreed. Well, I suppose we should get to bed. I have a feeling we'll both have busy days tomorrow."

"You're probably right, Young Me."

"But first, how do we get this glass off my hand?"

Upstairs, they brushed their teeth and changed into pajamas, quickly, wordlessly. (Actually, only Young Julian changed into pajamas, since Grown-up Julian didn't bring any from the future nor from the past.)

"Well, our escapades sure took a lot out of me. I think I'll get to bed," Grown-up Julian said, his hand on the ladder.

"Uh-uh," said Young Julian, pointing to the bottom bed.

"I'll pay you to let me sleep on the top bunk."

"How much?"

"Five dollars."

"Fine. You've got yourself a—Wait just a second. You said there's no money in the future. Show me the five dollars first."

"I'll sleep on the bottom."

CHAPTER 12

"Uh-oh!" were the first words Young Julian heard upon waking, which is rarely the ideal way to greet the day.

"What's wrong?" he asked, hopping down.

"I'm really low on charge. Really low—what the smart folks call 'critically.' If we don't figure this out by tomorrow..."

"What?"

"We'll be fighting over the top bunk for a long time."

"Not to mention, sooner or later future Mom and Dad are going to start worrying about you."

"I hadn't thought of that," Grown-up Julian said.

"We...*you* need to tell Dad."

"We can't."

"Why not?"

"I'll be grounded. Forever."

"You're twenty years old. That's, like, an adult. Almost. Sort of. They can't ground you."

"You do realize you're talking about *our* mom."

"Oh, yeah."

"There's got to be a way."

Young Julian stuck out his tongue a little, just off to the right, and bit it slightly, which he always did when thinking deeply—what the smart folks call "pondering." He looked up. Grown-up Julian was doing the same.

"Some things never change," he said.

"What?" said Grown-up Julian.

Young Julian copied—what the smart folks call "mimicked"—the thinking-tongue gesture. Both laughed.

"I guess maybe my future won't be so bad after all," Young Julian said. "After all, you're not so bad."

"Actually, it will be pretty good. You'll see. And thanks."

"So, what do we do?"

"Tell you what. I think I have enough charge to last until tomorrow. If we figure it out by...dinner-time, then we're all set."

"And if we don't?"

"Then, after dinner—and dessert—we go to Dad. Deal?"

"Deal. And today, try to stay off my bed while I'm gone."

"How did you know?"

"I have my ways," Young Julian said, pointing emphatically at the dreaded sub-bunk.

"Killjoy."

At school, with the morning's successful eTab-assisted end around on Biff and the inane pickle-cucumber conversation that preceded it now in all versions of the past, Julian settled in. As best as he could, all things considered. Because, really, now it was all downhill, since all he had to do was help his 20-year-old-self go back in time and undo a mistake that quite likely would pollute the natural timeline, rewrite history, and change the world as we know it.

At least.

What could go wrong?

The first period dragged. The second slogged. But then in the third...

Mrs. Stern had just begun her lesson.

"The Battle of Gettysburg was fought over three days, beginning on July 1st, 1863..."

Oh, that's funny—what the smart folks call "coincidental," thought Julian.

An on-and-off buzzing caught his attention. He leaned over, just a little so as not to draw the attention of Mrs. Stern, who almost never fell asleep while talking. He peeked into his backpack. Inside a faint green glow pulsed in sync with the buzz. He carefully placed two fingers into the rolled up eTab and spread them slightly, unrolling it just a bit.

"Julian? It's me. Can you hear me?"

He stiffened and looked around. It didn't seem as though anyone else had heard the inappropriately timed call.

Julian considered his options.

Quickly.

There was no way he could converse with himself in the classroom. A dash out the door would certainly lead to consequences. He needed an excuse.

He began coughing.

Cough, cough.

First just a little. Then louder and worse.

"Are you all right Julian?" Mrs. Stern asked.

"I just swallowed wrong. Can I go get a drink of water?"

"Of course. Come."

Slipping the eTab into his back pocket, Julian walked up to the front of the room, still coughing. She handed him a pass, his ticket out to the hall.

Julian ran over to the janitor's closet, which he knew was always unlocked, and slipped in.

He unrolled the eTab and swiped. Grown-up Julian's face appeared on the screen.

"Hi, Julian," he said gleefully.

"What are you doing? I'm kind of in class right now. What do you want?"

"I figured it out. I figured out the power source."

"You did!" Young Julian did his best to scream for joy. Silently. "What is it?"

"It's—Ooh! First, I need to tell you something really important."

"What could be more important than the power source?"

"It's about our future. Something you *need* to know."

"No way." Young Julian reached over and turned on a faucet. The rush of water saved him from hearing

Grown-up Julian say, "Forget the *Star Wars* LEGO sets. Buy two or three of *every* Abnormal Adolescent Samurai Salamander kit which comes out. And don't open the boxes. Ever. Put them away. In a safe place. Definitely keep them away from Dylan. And Dad. With what those things are going for on eBay, you'll be able to buy a house. A big house."

When Grown-up Julian's lips had stopped moving, Young Julian turned off the water.

Grown-up Julian shook his head. "I'm just trying to help, you know."

"I know. But don't."

"Where were we?"

"The power source."

"Yes, the power source. Are you ready?"

"Yes!"

"If I may boast, figuring it out was a pretty clever combination of investigative reporting and technical sleight-of-hand—what the realistic folks call 'a lucky break.' What I did was, I cross-referenced WikiEverything with the Dad Five-Minute Warning app, which let me read an encyclopedia of the future."

"That's very interesting. But I kind of snuck out of class, and right now I'm hiding in the janitor's closet, praying there are no spills in progress that would necessitate a mop. So if you don't mind, spill it!"

"Drum roll, please," Grown-up Julian said proudly. "It turns out Cucumium is pickles."

"Pickles?"

"Yes! Pickles."

"Pickles, as in..."

"Those green food things. Slices or spears. Dill or gherkin. Pickles."

"How can pickles be a source of energy?"

"Dad invented it."

"Say no more. What are you waiting for? Get some from the refrigerator and load it up. Or whatever you're supposed to do."

"There aren't any. Anywhere in the house. I looked."

"Seriously? What are the odds?"

"Well, for today, one hundred percent."

"Spare me the lesson in statisitics. Just run to the store and buy some."

"Money."

"What?"

"Remember, I said money is different in the future?"

"So?"

"So we don't have it. At least in coins or paper form."

"Did Mom leave her purse lying around? Because maybe you could find a few—"

"I thought about that. But she's got it alarmed, remember?"

"Um, no. No, I don't remember that."

"Oh. Then you'll find out the hard way. Someday."

"What do we do?" Young Julian asked, wiping a sweaty brow with a sweaty palm, all the while standing in sweaty socks and sneakers.

"What's for lunch today?"

"Lunch? Why?"

"Duh! I'm hungry. What's for lunch?"

"I think it's hamburgers."

"Perfect!"

"Why?"

"What goes with hamburgers?"

"Pickles!"

"Exactly," Grown-up Julian said, head turning, neck craning, eyes scanning Julian's room in search of a clock, oblivious to the fact that his own eTab had one in the lower right corner. "What time is recess? Noon?"

"12:15."

"How could I forget? So at lunch, get a few extra pickles. Then bring them out at recess. We can meet around the back of the building. You know, the parking lot overlooking the supermarket. In the little space between the dumpster and the wall."

"I think I know where you're talking about. How do you remember it?"

"Oh, you'll remember it, too. Because in a few years, that's the exact spot where you and Lisa Honeywell will..."

Grown-up Julian paused for effect. Or, just out of sheer cruelty.

"What!?"

"I'd better not say."

"*What*!?"

"I can't. I don't want to be responsible for—you know what I'm going to say—polluting the natural timeline. Can't tarnish the future now, can I?"

"Oh, come on!"

"Nope. You made your top bunk. And now you can sleep on it. In it. End of discussion." Grown-up Julian pantomimed pulling a zipper across his lips and then, for good measure, padlocking them, throwing away the key, and applying a length of duct tape.

"No fair."

Grown-up Julian shrugged. "Toodle-oo. See you at—"

A message scrolled across Grown-up Julian's screen.

YOUR ETAB IS GETTING LOW ON CHARGE. PLEASE PLUG IT IN RIGHT AWAY—WHAT THE SMART FOLKS CALL ASAP. GOING INTO STANDBY MODE. LOVE, DAD.

Then the screen went dark.

"Uh-oh," said Young Julian, now cut off from his older counterpart.

He walked slowly—what the smart folks call "trudged"—back to his classroom.

12:15 could not come soon enough.

CHAPTER 13

Julian inhaled his lunch. (A risky choice, as his mom often had to remind Dylan, the Human Vacuum Cleaner.) Wanting to keep the pickles safe and playground-dirt-free, he drank the last of his milk, carefully opened the empty carton fully, and placed the paper cup containing the pickles inside. He closed the carton back up and waited.

And waited.

And waited.

Finally, Mr. Warden, the lunchroom monitor and ~~Dungeon~~ Detention Master (a direct quote from the name tag that he alone among the teachers wore), announced they were free to go outside. Julian casually headed over to the door. He didn't want to be the first to go out, nor the last, and assumed an anonymous position somewhere within the middle of the pack. He walked out and hung around the playground, mingling with his classmates for a few minutes, before working his way to far end. He sat down on a swing and began swinging back...and forth...and back...and forth...

When Mr. Warden's back was turned, Julian executed a perfect slide-out maneuver at the top—what the smart folks call the "apex"—of his arc. He landed cleanly and dashed down the hill.

Grown-up Julian stood waiting for him.

"Hi. How's your day going?"

"Fine," Young Julian said. "Just the usual. Math. English. Biff trying to kill me."

"Typical, in other words."

"I suppose. Now about this thing with Lisa…"

"Forget it! I'm not saying a word. Other than, *Julian and Lisa, up in a tree. K-I*—OK, enough said. Did you get one?"

"I got a bunch," Young Julian said, opening the carton and removing—what the smart folks call "extracting"—the green fuel.

"Bananas grow in bunches. Pickles grow in barrels. Never mind," Grown-up Julian said, waving his hand as one does when shooing away an annoying gnat. "That joke was doomed from the start. All right, Young Me. Let's do this," said Grown-up Julian. He pushed a button on the eTab. A small panel raised out of the flatness of the face.

"Whoa!" said Young Julian. "Where did that come from?"

"I have no idea."

"It's like magic."

"Dad," they said in unison.

A small silver disk slipped out. Grown-up Julian took it and studied it.

"Hmmm," he said as a worried look crossed his face.

"What?"

"I need something sharp to open it," Grown-up Julian said.

"You didn't bring anything?"

"No."

"You didn't think to open it up, look at it, and see if you'd need a tool?"

"You know how I told you we're going to be clumsy? Well, we're going to be absent-minded, too."

"Great. *Now* what are we going to do?"

"Let me have the Swiss Army knife you always carry," Grown-up Julian said.

"How did you know I—Oh, yeah," he said, handing it over. "I'll never get used to that."

"In theory, after about two minutes you should never need to again. By the way...your blue tennis shoe."

"What?" asked Young Julian.

"You're going to lose that pocketknife for about six months. Look in your blue tennis shoe."

"You're not supposed to—"

"I don't think telling you where to find your own missing pocketknife is going to change the course of human history."

"You're probably right. *This* time."

"Got it," Grown-up Julian said as the silver lid popped off.

Sure enough, there was a dried—what the smart folks call "desiccated"—pickle in there. Grown-up

Julian tossed it aside. His younger self handed him a fresh one. He placed it in the center before replacing the lid.

"Well, here goes nothing," he said as he slid it back into the compartment, which disappeared into whatever invisible and inexplicable space it had come from.

He swiped. The eTab glowed. Brightly. Brilliantly. And the little power level icon—which both Julians could now clearly tell was a pickle—zipped up from 0.001% to 100%.

"Yes!"

"We did it!"

"We did, Young Me. High-five! A job well done. I could not have done this without you. Uh-oh!"

"What?"

"I lost my stylus!"

"Your what?

"Stylus. It's a small, pencil-like—"

"I know what a stylus *is*. The eTab doesn't have one."

"Mine does."

"Why? Why do you need one?"

"Why? Do you see how many numbers there are on my Dad Five-Minute Warning app? I needed something precise, so I hit the right date. The last thing I wanted do is fat-finger it and land in Pearl Harbor."

"You and your stupid *enhancements*. What do we do now?"

"I need something thin. Really thin. As thin as a human hair. But it's got to be hard. Really hard. Stiff."

Young Julian thought.

Quickly.

"I know just the thing. Give me my knife back. Wait here. And be ready. We're not going to have much time."

Clinging to the wall of the building, spy-like, Young Julian scooted around to the opposite side. Checking both ways, he sped across the parking lot, abandoning the school property, his second risky choice of the lunch hour. He eased along the chain-link fence that marked the border—what the smart folks call the "perimeter"—of the playground. His target loomed (and doomed) fifty feet ahead.

As he did every day, Biff, far too cool for kickball or basketball or football or foosball, was leaning against the other side of the very same fence, surveying his territory. With recess almost over, Julian knew he had to act now. He tiptoed up behind Biff, keeping a steady eye on his target all the while. But when he reached the base of Mount Masterson and strained to see the summit in the hazy distance, he was forced to put his plan on pause until he could find an elevator, or a Sherpa, or something that would fall into the general category of "tall thing." Spinning around, he scanned the area for anything to buy him a vertical foot or two.

He looked.

And looked.

And finally spied the prize!

Piled up behind the garage of the house that backed up to the school was a stack of logs. The perfect one, a foot wide and eighteen inches high, laid there. The angelic voices started singing once more (though in fairness, the choir was practicing extra in preparation for the fall show). He rolled it carefully and quietly over to the fence, directly behind Biff. Julian worked hard—what the smart folks call "labored"—to stand it on end, then climbed on the top. He took out his knife and opened the little springy scissor tool. With his other hand he pulled out the Swiss Army tweezers and carefully, oh so carefully, reached them through the fence. He grasped the tip of one of Biff's hair spikes. Julian maneuvered the scissors through a link several inches below and...

Snip!

"Hey! What do you think you're doing?" Biff said, swiveling around. Seeing Julian holding one of his laboriously lubed-up locks, he growled, if a rhinoceros could growl. "Pickle! You got away from me this morning. But not this time!"

Now it was off to the races, as Biff and his buddies would be chasing Julian as soon as they could get to his side of the chain-link fence. Luckily, Julian knew that, just like a locomotive engine, Biff took a while to get going. Unfortunately, once Biff started moving, there was no stopping him.

Young Julian zipped back to where Grown-up Julian was hiding, covering the last fifty yards in a time which would have made Mr. Stringbean, the track coach, proud.

"Here," Young Julian said, handing over the tweezers. "Will this work?"

"I think so."

"Great. Hurry."

"Why?"

"Don't ask. Just hurry," Young Julian said as he listened for the sound of the oncoming stampede.

"OK, June 30, 1863," Grown-up Julian said, entered the precious digits. "And here we—"

"Wait!" yelled Young Julian.

"What?"

"Didn't the Battle of Gettysburg begin on July 1st?"

"Yes! You *were* paying attention. I'm so glad. We're on our way. Now then...three...two—"

"Wait!"

"What?"

"So why are you going back to June 30?"

The distant rumble began reaching Julian's ears.

"Because I'll never be able to find my cell phone on that battlefield. I mean, it was loud, and smoky, and—I did mention bullets were flying, didn't I?"

"Yes, but—"

"Do you really think I'm going to crawl around on all fours *looking* for it?"

"I suppose that would be pretty stupid."

"I suppose it would. So, what I'm going to do is go back to the day before and wait for myself to show up. And when I do, I'm going to tell myself to just leave it in my pocket, and not bother with any pictures. That way, I can't lose it."

"Won't it be weird? Going back to the middle of the Civil War and seeing yourself there?" Young Julian asked.

"Any weirder than this?" said Grown-up Julian, pointing first at himself, then his younger self, and once more at each of them for good measure.

"I guess not."

The leaves on the trees above them began rustling, even though it was a windless afternoon.

"Do you feel something?"

"Something like the ground beneath our feet shaking, as if an earthquake were about to come around the corner behind me and rattle the teeth out of our mouths?"

"Yeah."

"No. I don't. Now hurry."

"OK. Goodbye, Young Me. And good luck." Grown-up Julian tapped the screen. The vacuum cleaner sound covered the growing storm. "I think it's going to work!" said Grown-up Julian. "I can't thank you enough."

"We sure turned out OK."

"We did. One last thing. Microwave butter pop-corn, and flypaper."

"What?"

"Microwave butter popcorn and flypaper. Remember them. Sorry."

"No!"

"And a sling sh—" Grown-up Julian disappeared in a flash of light.

Young Julian breathed a well-deserved sigh of relief. Unfortunately, his relief was brief.

"Hey!" the voice behind him yelled.

He turned.

Biff's fist, coming at his eye, was the last thing Julian remembered seeing.

That evening, back at home, Julian sat alone in his room, grateful Grown-up Julian had stashed—what the smart folks call "surreptitiously placed"—a small tube of Shiner-B-Gone in his pocket. He would have had a hard time explaining to his mom why he'd gotten a black eye.

He opened the old, dusty footlocker he had found in the attic and dragged down to his room after school. On it, he had taped a sign.

BEWARE!
STRANGE—WHAT THE SMART FOLKS CALL UNPREDICTABLE—OBJECTS INSIDE.

Julian chose the plural form of the word "object" because he somehow knew—what the smart folks call "suspected"—this would not be the last of his dad's misbehaving inventions.

He placed the eTab inside, shut the lid, clicked the padlock closed, and put the key on a chain that he then slipped around his neck. Then he went downstairs to what he hoped would be a normal dinner.

If such a thing were possible in the Newcomber house.

END

ACKNOWLEDGEMENTS

I would like to thank...

My wonderful wife Jean, who tolerates this mental illness of mine called "writing"

My children, who may or may not resemble the Newcomber kids

The Village of Chagrin Falls, which definitely resembles Whispering Falls, and hopefully someday will serve as the filming location for the screen adaptation

And all the folks at Common Deer Press, who believed in this wacky enterprise

ABOUT

Michael Seese has published three books: *Haunting Valley*, a collection of fictional ghost stories centered around his home town; *Scrappy Business Contingency Planning*, which teaches corporate BCP professionals how to prepare for bad things; and *Scrappy Information Security*, which teaches us all how to keep the cyber-criminals away. He was inspired to write *eTab* after countless readings of the Junie B. Jones series to his children. Other than that, Michael spends his spare time rasslin' with the young'uns.

Visit www.MichaelSeese.com or follow @MSeeseTweets to laugh with him or at him.

a jewish journal of thought and culture

fall/winter, 2005

FROM THE EDITORS

It's sometimes said that Judaism, at least as practiced today, is a religion of time rather than space. Our Biblical ancestors venerated holy places in Jerusalem and elsewhere, but today the pious build, in Heschel's phrase, "cathedrals in time," and sanctify moments on the calendar more than locations in geography.

Yet the pull of physical place is irresistible, as evidenced both by recent current events and the preoccupations in this sixth issue of Zeek's print edition. We look homeward with ambivalence, nostalgia, and ideology; we note how a sense of place is constituted by communities and imagination as much as by geography; and we wrestle with the dynamic between sacred *mekomot,* nodes of being which have ineluctable significance for our emotional or spiritual selves, and the monotheistic impulse toward *ha-makom,* the Place which is always present. From David Ehrlich's ambivalence to the passion captured in Kitra Cahana's photographs, and from the diasporism of British Muslims to the all-too-significant centrality of the Kotel, the places evoked in these pages resonate, summon, and challenge us.

Zeek, because it is in part an online publication, can itself sometimes seem separated from the physical geography of planet Earth. Yet our contributors, editors, subscribers, and readers are a dynamic community, one that is growing at a surprisingly rapid pace. With this issue, we would like to welcome our new fiction editor, Joshua Furst, acknowledge the generous support of the Dorot Foundation and the National Foundation for Jewish Culture, and invite you to subscribe to our journal either online at www.zeek.net or using the form at the back.

Finally, as we consider questions of space, place, and home, we would like to wish you a winter of no boundaries - only ever-widening horizons.

Jay Michaelson	Bara Sapir	Dan Friedman
Michael Shurkin	Leah Koenig	Joshua Furst

Z E E K

Zeek is an independent Jewish journal of thought and culture, published by Metatronics Inc. Founded in 2002, Zeek is devoted to an integral vision of Jewish culture and spirit, and to publishing new poetry and prose that reflects the breadth and depth of Jewish experience and concerns. New content appears online every month at www.zeek.net. Printed versions appear twice a year. Zeek is a project of the National Foundation for Jewish Culture, and is supported by the Dorot Foundation.

JAY MICHAELSON   CHIEF EDITOR
DAN FRIEDMAN   ASSOCIATE EDITOR
BARA SAPIR   ART EDITOR
JOSHUA FURST   FICTION EDITOR
MICHAEL SHURKIN ASSISTANT EDITOR
LEAH KOENIG   ASSISTANT EDITOR
ADVISORY BOARD: ROGER BENNETT, JENNIFER BLEYER, NEIL GORDON, RABBI JILL HAMMER, STEVE JACOBSON, AMICHAI LAU-LAVIE, RABBI MICHAEL PALEY, NIGEL SAVAGE

Subscriptions: $25/two years (four issues). Checks should be made to Metatronics Inc. Payment accepted online, which we prefer. Non-US subscriptions add $10/year for postage.
Submissions: Submissions of art, poetry, essays, fiction, and criticism are welcome, via email only to zeek @zeek.net.
Contact: Zeek Magazine, 104 West 14th Street, 4th Floor, New York, NY 10011. Email (strongly preferred): zeek@zeek.net.
Distribution: Ubiquity Distribution, 607 Degraw St., Brooklyn NY 11217
p: 718-875-5491 f: 718-875-8047
Back issues are available on amazon.com and www.zeek.net.

ISSN # 1548-2103
ISBN # 1-932400-06-0
Cover photograph: Julie Dermansky

Please visit us online at **www.zeek.net**.

Everything's Fine

DAVID EHRLICH

TRANSLATED BY BEN LERMAN

Once a month, according to the Hebrew calendar, Mom and
Dad write me a letter from Israel. Here in Moab, Utah, I
tear open the envelope with my fingers, too rushed to look
for a knife, and lay a small pile of news on the kitchen
counter. First is a detailed portrait of the weather in Mom's
fine, precise hand. After that come the stories about the
grandchildren, and then the uncles and the aunts, and in the
end a little news from the yard.

The mulberry tree is sick.

I close my eyes and imagine the little courtyard in
Holon, the way it looks from the round table on the porch.
I see every leaf, every grasshopper and beetle. We used to
have some sad, reddish flowers that could never adapt to
the harsh soil, but my father, a strong man, fussed over
them in his stubborn way and kept them alive ten bitter
years.

Till they died on him.

The grass survives. Dad waters it four times a week
- at night, to save on water. He stands with the red hose
and directs it carefully, apportioning the stream correctly
and justly. He won't put a sprinkler in the yard, just as he
won't bring a television set into the house. Alone, lit by a
pale triangle of light from the porch, he waters the heavy
soil, and a feeling of creativity comes over him.

His son up and left for America, but the grass stayed
behind, helpless and faithful and still turning green from
year to year, despite the fact that the son's return looks ever
more doubtful.

If there is bad news, Mom hides it at the end,

towards the close of the letter, to soften the blow. "Nimrod's grandfather had a heart-attack but now he's OK." I lift my gaze to the top of the mountain out the window. I always loved Nimrod's grandfather, not having had a grandfather of my own. And now, go figure what happened to him and when. Mom, in her efforts to send me a healthy and pleasant picture of Israel, won't provide more detail. At the end of the page her handwriting is strong and optimistic, and she describes, in her traditional paragraph, the approach of spring.

And then comes Dad, in strong letters drawn with strokes that tail off as if refusing to quit. He corrects Mom's predictions of the weather in the appropriate places, grumbles about work, and signs off with the standard line: "And all the rest Mom has already written." Sometimes he plants a solitary island of emotion: "We thought about you today," or even "We miss you," always in the plural.

This time there is also a P.S.: "We thought we might possibly come to visit you in December, if it works out."

I put the letter down in shock. A parental visit in Moab, Utah. For a moment I try to see them entering the rusty gate and struggling with the screen door, but I can't.

Again I read the letter. We thought we might possibly come to visit you in December, if it works out. Three qualifiers in one line. It wasn't money or distance or health that dictated those qualifiers. It was our tense relationship, layers of trepidation and pain, suspicion and grievance, untranslated love and years of frustration. Through all that, they don't have a clue if I want them to come, and neither do I.

* * *

Since the letter I haven't been able to see a single thing without thinking, What will they say.

Jay Michaelson

My room for example.

A rug and a wicker table and an old armchair and two posters of landscapes, one of nearby Arches National Monument, and the second of the Banias back home.

Dad will ask why I don't buy myself a desk.

In my room I lie down and listen to Joni Mitchell, whose sad notes make my autumn depression a little sweet. With her I manage to see outside myself, to boundless blue vistas, into her longing.

Mom would hear ten seconds of the song and say, Why is she yelling, this woman? I close my eyes and listen to the cassette. The words, in a language not my own, don't connect, but the syllables have a life of their own, hovering in space, abstract.

Now the song I love. It calms me enough that my mind wanders, only to return with the next song. And not alone, but with a boy, pleasing and fair, who lies down in my bed and dreams my dreams with me.

Dad will ask, Do you have a girlfriend yet, and I will smile with difficulty and tell him no, and Mom will stare at him and at me with a confused look, a look both accused and accusing. And we will never go further.

In the evening I'll go to Betsy's for a cup of tea. Betsy is almost seventy-seven, and she has acres of curly hair and a porch with three chairs upholstered in yellow, where she sits and looks back on her life. She and I have nothing in common aside from this tea and her memory, which, sparked by my curiosity, takes off, flutters about, and alights in the least expected places, and then her face softens as if returning to a former self. The porch darkens and a reddish-blue band of light descends on the rock that looks like a giant bird. Only then does Betsy make the tea and lay out dinner for me. On her table the stories pile up, suffused with a desert aroma.

Mom will say, What business do you have with this old lady, She could be your grandmother.

And then I will have to explain to them what I'm doing here.

I won't tell everything. I'm not sure that I understand, myself. I'll show them the flyers about rafting. I'll take them to the cabin on the banks of the Colorado River. I'll introduce them to old Donald, who gave me work on the boats three years ago, when I happened on this place during a cross-country trip. He'll murmur to them and they'll murmur back in Hebrew.

Everything I say will sound unconvincing, as if there were no breaking the wall of their doubt and mistrust, and under Dad's demanding gaze I will shrink and shrink, and in the end nothing will remain of me but a small bubble of apology, a crumb, then nothing.

* * *

At six I get up to clean the room. At this blessed hour the specks of dust have a special radiance, but Mom and dust are ancient enemies, and I mobilize against it with her methods, which don't help but only bestow on it another, almost spiritual quality. I know that Mom won't accept graciously that dust has any good points. Without looking at me she'll chase away with an iron hand the specks that have escaped and will leave my room pure and clean.

With the morning sun I hang a sign in the entrance, "Welcome Mom and Dad." Three times I move the flowers, trying to give my hovel the appearance of a home. The pink carnations look a little confused.

I put by the beds two maps of the area next to the bed, and pause for a moment. Mom and Dad in my bed in Utah. I think of them in the old bed in Holon. I remember playing between them on Saturday mornings. I can't imagine them in my bed, and I go outside where the sun has grown stronger.

Why look at this as a nightmare, I demand of

myself. And from the headquarters of the pain, I send out an order not to be angry, only to love - for a week, anyway.

I turn the vase, so that the flowers will enjoy the glow of the desert, and it's as if I'm offended in advance by the thought that Mom and Dad won't even notice them. I put them back.

* * *

It's not that I don't want to write; it just doesn't work for me. You know that I don't write. Even from the army I didn't write to you. If I had money I would call. I know that you understand, but I'm just explaining.

And also, what am I going to write? About the boats? About the weather? I have nothing to write.

I actually tried to start a few times. Just a couple of months ago, when I got the letter that you were coming, I sat an entire evening where Mom is sitting now and I tried to write. But nothing came out . Writing is not my thing. What can I do.

I look at the flowers, and they don't answer me. In vain, I rehearse dialogues of things I'll never say.

* * *

When they come, they are waiting for me (I'm late) on the light blue plastic chairs under the "Arrivals" sign, pale and worried. Even when I reach them the worry doesn't go away. Because this worry goes all the way back to Abraham, and no reasoning is going to uproot it. In Steve's Cafe, two days later, Dad drums with his fork on the table, and casually asks, Nu, what's with the girls here, and Mom surprises me: apparently prepared for this moment, she says Moshek, don't ask too much. When he has something to announce, he'll say so. And Dad, not pleased with the interruption, throws her a look, glances down at his fork, drums a bit more and concludes: Yes, yes. Yes, yes.

When it's all over, the moment of parting arrives at the place where the baggage carts are parked. We don't say anything important, worn out by each other but not wanting to take leave of each other, stuck in a fixed trap. The tears burst out at the end, after they've disappeared, pale and old, with the last of the travelers at the gate, and a last goodbye wave has died in the closing door of the elevator. And then, to the roar of the engines warming up, I understand that we can only be close when we're far apart.

* * *

Dear Oren,

We got back three days ago, and, as usual after trips, we're asking ourselves if we were really in America. It was a little warm on Monday, but when we saw Miri and Gili, we forgot everything. They made us open the suitcases before we even left the airport (by the way, they've changed the whole arrangement at the airport, you wouldn't recognize it at all). Gili is happy with the sneakers despite the fact that they are a tiny bit big on him.

The yard wasn't in the best condition. Your brother said he'd watered it, but Dad will have to work hard to get the grass back in shape. On Saturday the whole family is coming, and also Menachem from Hadera. It seems to me he hasn't been here for two years, since the last Seder we made, that you weren't at. And Naphtali and Ella may come too. We hope we'll have the slides from the trip back by then. Other than that, there's nothing new. Look after yourself, and buy yourself a sweater like we said.

Kisses,

Mom

Shalom Oren,

Mom has written everything there is to tell. The yard will be all right. With a little effort and some late winter rain everything will be back to normal. I'm attaching a few articles about the political situation. If you like we'll get you a subscription to the newspaper, so you'll know what's going on.

Kisses,

Dad

* * *

It's turned cool. I ride my bike along the banks of the river and turn onto Highway 55. My eyes are fixed on the white stripe at the edge, focused so hard that I don't realize it's getting dark.

Suddenly I think about Mom. How much I would like to sit with her on the porch and eat grapes.

Highway 55 forks. There is something relaxing in this well-numbered, well-marked system, and it gives you the illusion that you know where you're going.

In the fading light I turn onto a road that isn't numbered. I strain my muscles, cut through air and water, gather every possible longing into the basket on the front of my bike, strengthen my grip on the handlebars, suck air into my cheeks and blow it out, and while my legs keep up their pedaling, I am wrapped in fog and glide through it with the confidence of being on automatic pilot. I feel the chill and the salty mist. My eyes close for a second, and in my head a tune plays from my childhood. I emerge from the gray into the roundabout at the entrance to the town, and my tired legs accelerate one last time, and in this way I slip into our yard, almost falling over the red hose Dad is using to water the lawn in the dark, and I drop the bike against the porch steps. Inside, Mom is reading the newspaper, and she raises her eyes and studies me with simple affection, not surprised, and I lay my head on her bosom and say almost voicelessly, "Now it's all right, it's all right now."

And she caresses me and nods her head.

Joyce Ellen Weinstein, *Shifra and Puah*

The Place of Ashes

JILL HAMMER

"The priest shall carry it to a clean place outside the camp, to where the ashes (*deshen*) are poured out, and burn it up on a wood fire; it shall be burned on the ash heap."   Leviticus 4:12

"Humans shelter in the shadow of your wings; they feed on the abundance (*deshen*) of your house."
Psalms 36:9

You burn all the names;
the forest of them goes up like a torch of branches.
You are brittle leaves; you crumble where I step.
You are a woman with drifting limbs;
I reach for your warm skin, and your arm dissolves.
I am dry moss to you; in an instant eaten to nothing.

I am the priestess of the ash heap.
I will let feathers from the fire sift through my fingers
and speak to each ember prayers it understands.
I will eat the ashes of your house
and go naked among the wreaths of air,
for no breastplate could signify you,
and no twelve stones could combine to tell
the heat of your shadow-colored wings
or trace the labyrinth of your hair.

The Last Days of Gaza

PHOTOGRAPHS BY KITRA CAHANA

Jewish Gaza is history. Whether there ever was a religious or strategic reason for Jews to be in the historic land of the Philistines, is now an academic question. The "Disengagement" process threatened to tear Israel apart, but it didn't. Though Jerusalem was festooned with orange banners and posters decrying "national suicide" and likening the disengagement to the Holocaust, for most people, life went on as normal.

But for a sizable minority, Summer 2005 was a political, and theological, catastrophe. Thousands of people thought God would save them from evacuation. But God chose otherwise, and the time of reflection has only just begun.

Photographer Kitra Cahana spent most of the two months leading up to disengagement in Gaza, recording thousands of images of a now-vanished community. (A larger selection of her work is featured on our online edition.) These images, mostly of children - Israeli soldiers being, in large part, teenagers themselves - are interesting to contemplate. Whatever the political context, the kids seem innocent, and trapped. Then again, they are lucky compared with tho ones on the other side of the fence.

Will a truly autonomous Palestinian Authority reduce the threats of violence, or increase them? Is Gaza a prelude, or a subterfuge? Only fools and zealots say that they know.

Really, the "last days of Gaza" are the first days of Gaza. Some of the settlements were like paradise - but they came at the price of blood. Now they are gone, and the people in these images have all gone elsewhere. Have they retreated only to fight another day? Or might life outside the Gaza Strip give them a taste of the ordinary? As in the poem by Yehuda Amichai, redemption appears in unexpectedly boring places.

- Eds.

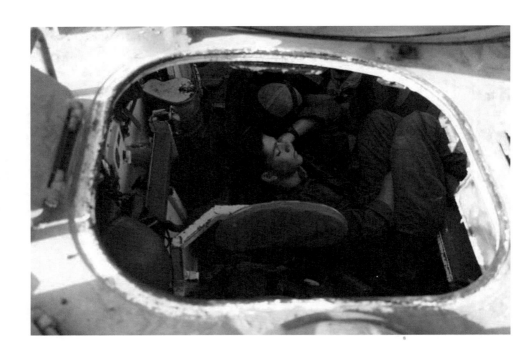

Dear God

REBECCA MOSTOV

At the Kotel,
people write notes to God
and stick them between the stones.

You can't help but be tempted
to open and read them,
different languages,
from tourists, rabbis, children:

Dear God,
My mom made me do this.
I think it's dumb.

They bulge through crevices,
spill over onto the ground,
crumpled wishes
torn from notebooks
or separated neatly
from decorated stationery pads.

Dear God,
There's this girl...

Some are folded into triangles,
like passing notes
before 5th period.
Maybe He opens them
under a desk,
excited for gossip.

Dear God,
What were you thinking...

People squint under Jerusalem sun,
wiping sweat from their necks,
kneeling to make shadows
as they write.

Ethan Backer

The So-Called Jewish Cultural Revolution

LEAH KOENIG

1. The Good Bad Kids

Scene 1: Somewhere in the maze-like bowels of the massive United Jewish Communities federation building in New York City. I'm sitting in a three-walled cubicle that is home to JDub Records - a non-profit Jewish record and event production company. I am with JDub recording artist Josh Dolgin, also known as So Called: the Yiddish-rapping, accordion-wielding, Klezmer hip hop maestro. I have half an hour of his time, and an under-prepared list of interview questions.

Several minutes into the interview, we are interrupted by a 30-something UJC employee, who appears around a corner wearing his compulsory shirt and tie.

> Random Employee: Hey man, I've seen you play!
> So Called: Come on now...
> RE: I did! A couple of months ago in Brooklyn - you play the accordion, right?
> SC: I'm that guy.
> RE: Oh dude, you were great. (Reflective pause.) Except for the "Baruch atah adonai, mother f--ker." You wrote that, right? That wasn't so beautiful.

The employee babbles on as Josh reveals to me that he wrote that "blessed" line in tenth grade - one of his first raps. Suddenly a light comes into the interview-crasher's eye:

> RE: Do you know where you are dude? Do you understand what building you're in?

This is So Called

SC: Sort of...

RE: It's like a crazy Jewish conspiracy...

Scene 2: The Lower East Side's Slipper Room - home of JDub Record's monthly party series, Slivovitz and Soul, which was created for, and features, So Called. The room is lit with red bulbs and crowded with Jewish-hipster hybrids. A group of Hasids cluster near the glittery bar, and one or two confused-looking blond girls click their stilettos impatiently. The bartender hands out free shots of Slivovitz plum brandy, and a back table holds copies of So Called's long-awaited album, *The So Called Seder: A Hip-Hop Haggadah.*

So Called is busy on stage rocking the party - his voice rippling over Yiddish melodies, punctuated by a few solid horn players and anchored by his accordion playing and funky beats. A group of the less-inhibited hipsters dance a clumsy and spirited hora. A couple of boys with Jew-fros watch in smiling (almost) disbelief at the unexpected harmony of Yiddish and hip hop. Their friends groove near the stage - eyes closed, sweating.

Around 11:45pm I am approached by a casual looking guy in dark jeans who I assume wants to exercise his J-date skills (And why not? There was already rampant Jew-to-Jew flirting going on in the room).

My Bashert: "Pardon me, can I ask you a question?"

Me: Hmmm? Oh, sure.

B: Well, actually a couple of questions. I'm doing a study on the people who come to events like this.

Me: I would love to - wait. You're what?

B: Yeah, I have this grant from the National Foundation of Jewish Culture to research the types of people who are attracted to shows like this.

Me: Excuse me, I have to go to the bathroom.

What do these two scenes have in common? First, they highlight So Called's growing reputation as an artist who has tapped into Jewish music's inner funkaliciousness. So Called's fans seem equally pleased by the explicit "Jewishness" of his music as they are by his fresh beats. There is little doubt that if So Called had said to the Slivovitz audience "when I say cool, you say Jew," there would be an enthusiastic chorus of: Cool! Jew! Cool! Jew!

Perhaps the oddest thing that ties the scenes together, however, is not So Called or grooving Jews, but the presence of the mainstream Jewish funding in So Called's decidedly fringe scene. Throughout the last half-decade, the Jewish federation system and some of the mega-philanthropists (think or google UJA Federation, United Jewish Communities, Bronfman, Steinhardt, Schusterman...) started to invest increasing amounts of energy and money into the cultivation of Jewish culture. More specifically, they have invested the money into the cultivation of Jews, using culture as the fertilizer. They know that many contemporary young Jews do not find Judaism to be relevant to their lives, interests, or identities. They are frustrated by the pandemic of Jews who have distanced themselves from anything Jewish. And if culture works, they're for it.

At the same time, the last half-decade has given way to a number of Jewish artists like So Called and Matisyahu (JDub's other musical sensation), as well as a growing cadre of innovative Jewish organizations, publications, websites, blogs, funding networks, and companies. These organizations - like Heeb magazine, the Jewish-environmental organization Hazon (for which I work), the ritual theatre company Storahtelling, and Zeek (for which I also work) - are breathing the spirit of contemporary life into Judaism and the ruach of Judaism into contemporary life. (Of course, not all the "new Jewish organizations" are equally hip and Jewishly substantive - some enterprises are indeed one and not the other). Mainline federations and philanthropists, in turn, have noticed that artists like So Called get their little Rachels and Noahs - who formerly renounced their Hebrew school upbringing - dancing to a Jewish beat, in a way their own heavily-funded but seriously lame efforts cannot. Thus, the shift in federation thinking (and giving) towards things "young, innovative and Jewish" is beginning to peek through the cracks of establishment. They don't really get it, but the kids like it, and so... fine.

In the last few years, there have been a spate of incubators for Jewish cultural creatives - efforts like the Joshua Venture, cohorts across the world, and programs like Bikkurim, in whose space I was sitting when I interviewed So Called. JDub Records is among the Bikkurim-sponsored groups, along with Hazon. Heeb and Storahtelling graduated from Bikkurim residencies and now are self-sustainable non-profits. Ten years ago, the likelihood that So Called would have been sitting in the organizational heart of mainstream Jewish philanthropy would be slim to none. But there he was - an innovative Jewish musician, produced by a ground-breaking Jewish organization, and being interviewed for a progressive Jewish journal.

It would be difficult - ridiculous actually - for Hazon or any of the other Bikkurim groups to complain about free office space. But sometimes my coworkers at Hazon and I joke that we are like misbehaving stepchildren who are begrudgingly invited to a family gathering, with UJC cast in the role of the over-authoritative parent not letting us "do what we want." Although, in this case, we want to help build inclusive Jewish community, not smoke in the bathroom.

On the micro-level, culture clashes are inevitable, though not serious. Last summer, for example, one of Hazon's summer interns came to work in a short denim skirt and tank top; the next day, another staff member walked into the office sweaty from his bike ride to work and holding a helmet (again, perfectly acceptable - especially considering Hazon runs organized Jewish environmental bike rides). By Friday, an embarrassing e-mail was sent out to the entire UJC floor reminding employees of appropriate attire. The email did not specifically name names, but among the outlined no-nos were mini skirts, shoulder-bearing tops, and sports clothes.

More serious clashes have also erupted - as when *Heeb* was accused of being anti-Zionist, and then pornographic, by a few funders who didn't seem to get the joke. For its part, Zeek has been ludicrously labeled a "gay magazine" by more than one Jewish organization, even though fewer than 5% of its articles have any gay themes, and sexual orientation has never been part of our mission statement. Presumably one gay article (or editor) is enough to taint the lot.

Personally, I am consistently amazed and humbled that as a 23 year old who graduated college last year, I can make such a significant difference in the trajectory of an organization, like Hazon or Zeek. UJC's larger corporate office, conversely, often feels like an old boys club. So, as the number of other innovative Jewish upstarts begins to swell, I can't help but wonder what our larger place in the mainstream Jewish world will actually be. Does our influx herald a coming triumph for American Jewish culture and community? Or are we merely an experimental line-item to a philanthropic world weary of underperforming blue-chips and ready for some dot-com?

2. The Real Deal?

So Called is certainly amongst the measured triumphs of the new Jewish culture. His background is instructive. Like many Jewish youngsters, Josh Dolgin did not grow up listening to Yiddish music, nor did he have any strong connection to Judaism. "I hated Hebrew school," he told me. "I learned how to read this language but not understand it. It all seemed kind of silly to me. My family would go to our synagogue for high holidays - I wasn't really into it."

From a young age, however, Josh was really into music. He started with classical piano, but it was through his connections with a salsa band during high school that Josh began to get into gospel music as well as the sequencing, sampling, and beat making that members of the gospel band he joined were doing in their basements.

Before long, Josh started experimenting with making his own beats and soon realized that he needed musical fuel for his fire. He began to search local thrift stores and alleyways for records that he could pull samples from. "This was over ten years ago when people were just throwing out their records," he said. "I would just take them out of the garbage and bring them to my house." Not surprisingly, a number of the 5,000 records Josh collected during the last decade were Klezmer and Yiddish records that people had thrown out. Two of the first he remembers finding were Mickey Katz's *Music for Weddings, Bar*

Mitzvahs, and Brisses and *Aaron Lebedeff sings Fourteen Yiddish Theatre Classics.*

As the adage goes, other people's trash turned out to be Josh's treasure. "I'd always thought that Jewish music sucked because it was corny, Debbie Friedman crap. But these records were just full of these little breakdowns and sounds that I could use, so I started to seek them out more than others." Over time, Josh started to develop the signature sound for which So Called is known. "It was hip hop that really got me into learning traditional Yiddish songs. Which is kind of insane."

So Called has not been content to take his discovery of Jewish music at face value. "I'm not just slapping a Jewish melody on top of a beat," he said. "I'm actually learning the stuff from the bottom up." The attention to technique, language, and tradition has paid off. Listening to So Called play an accordion or sing in Yiddish, one would swear that he was raised a century ago on the Lower East Side - in a good way. So Called's sincere interest in learning the music has brought him into contact with some of the remaining klezmer music all-stars, like Elaine Hoffman Watts, the 75-year old Yiddish drummer from Philadelphia. "I sample her all the time," So Called said. "She is playing the music she learned from her father. It's this amazing funky beat that no one ever hears." So what do So Called's teachers think of the hip hop twist he incorporates with their traditional tunes? "My showing interest in this culture is what makes [them] happy," he says. "They're okay with [my doing something new], as long as I'm respecting it."

So Called's audience seems to pick up on and appreciate his "not-your-bubbe's-music" kitsch appeal. But So Called has come a long way from his first "*baruch atah adonai* mother f--ker" rapping attempts, and being kitschy is not the point. The point, So Called insists, is to get people to dance. To have fun, to feel something - the way that all good hip hop (and klezmer) can.

JDub Records executive director Aaron Bisman says

that JDub's mission is to "create community and foster positive Jewish identity among young Jews, their friends, and significant others by promoting proud, authentic Jewish voices in popular culture and through cross cultural musical dialogue." (This elevator pitch sounds remarkably similar to Hazon's, Zeek's, Storahtelling's etc. pitches in that it promises the strengthening and enlarging of Jewish community.) In bringing diverse but distinctly Jewish music to the public, JDub is seeking to "revision the boundaries and categories of Judaism that we have gotten to know." In other words, Jewish music does not have to be "corny, Debbie Friedman crap" and Jewishness does not have to be experienced only in synagogues, or in ways that are irrelevant or ostracizing to Jews who do not fit into the molds of tradition. By expanding and reshaping Jewish boundaries, JDub has begun to validate and even popularize "out" Jewish music to a population of Jews who would otherwise have nothing to do with it. Likewise, Heeb, Hazon, and Storahtelling - not to mention Zeek - serve as gateways through which Jews can discover that Judaism's ancient wisdom need not be hidden in ancient packaging. At least in theory.

Bisman describes So Called's music as "spot on" what JDub is trying to do. Although So Called works closely with traditional Jewish music and is the musical director at an Orthodox synagogue (yes, really), his own relationship to Judaism does not fit into traditionally defined categories. "I don't believe in God and I don't believe in religion," he said. So Called's connection with Judaism - something he admits he is still figuring out - was sparked by his deep love and respect of both hip hop and of his Jewish predecessors like Hoffman Watts and Mickey Katz. He realized that, "hip hop is about representing who you are and your crew. When I started making this type of music I didn't really have an identity. I was just this little weird Jewish kid. Then I realized hey, that's who I am."

That Jewish funders have begun to tune into the work

Andy Alpern

of self-identified "weird Jewish kids" and innovative organizations is commendable - if a little surprising. One wonders to what extent they "get it" and to what extent desperation is driving them to try this new idea even despite deep skepticism of it. Certainly, when that skepticism is reinforced - when Heeb runs another provocative cover image, for example - there have been sharp reactions in some quarters. Can they put up with So Called's atheism if he brings their kids together? Should they? Should Jewish funders hold their nose and believe the focus groups?

For a small, innovative upstart organization, the financial backing of the established funding community ensures both financial support and an implied sense of organizational legitimacy. (Zeek, incidentally, benefits from the support of the Dorot Foundation and the National Foundation for Jewish Culture.) However, one cannot help but wonder if there is a catch. Do the joys of being a little fringe and under the radar get somehow cheapened with a federation's stamp of approval? Does a federation's logo at a Slivovitz and Soul show elicit the same wince as the Verizon logo gracing the program of a jazz festival? Even as someone deeply involved in the Jewish upstart world - who knows the realities of working with big foundations - I still cringe when I am handed a participant satisfaction survey at a Jewish cultural event. Maybe, though, we should just get over it - just as most people have gotten over the Verizon logo and learned to enjoy the music. Or maybe the right model, given that so many of the dollars in the Jewish community come from private sources, is less the Verizon Jazz Festival than the return of artistic patronage. Some of the Medicis "got" Leonardo and Michelangelo. Others didn't. But they all supported the culture.

One significant difference between this round of patronage and earlier ones (from the Medicis forward) is the role of the focus groups and questionnaires. The Medicis, arguably, funded culture they considered beautiful. Today's foundations fund art they consider effective - effective at attracting and retaining new Jews. Really, they might not care if So Called doesn't believe in God, or if *Heeb* is sacrilegious (actually, some of the most noted Jewish philanthropists are self-identified atheists, so disbelief is probably a plus). If the focus groups say that kids like it, then more power to them. For those of us on the upstart side who care deeply about the work we are doing, this realization can be difficult to swallow.

In the details, focus group methodology varies. Some foundation-funded surveys simply measure whether more Jews are doing Jewish-y activities like going to Slilovitz and Soul shows. If they show up, and (hopefully) meet other Jews, then great. Other studies are more ambitious, and try to gauge if Jews are being engaged enough by their "new Jewish encounters" to continue their exploration beyond the front gate. But what happens if the sociologist's surveys from scene two turn up with unsatisfactory results? In a sense, if So Called, Matisyahu, *Heeb, Zeek*, or Storahtelling are asked to compromise, it's no different from when large publishers or record labels order their artists to produce a hit, or not rock the boat. There are mixed motives, but this, too, is like the mainstream of American media: independent artists and musicians are often in the business to make the best art they can, while the people writing the checks are looking at the bottom line. The only difference is the metric; in the record industry, it's sales - in Jewish philanthropy, it's souls.

The amount of money allocated to Jewish upstarts - though significantly more than ten years ago - is still miniscule, as a share of total Jewish philanthropy. Bikkurim's website says, "Since its founding in 2000, Bikkurim has provided over a half million dollars in in-kind support to a total of 16 new Jewish organizations." That's an average of $30,000 per organization. In comparison, UJC allotted ten million dollars in summer 2005 alone to fund Israeli summer camps. And even that was a drop in the Jewish funding bucket. These are organizations with billion-dollar budgets, and it's an open secret in the Jewish organizational world that several well-subsidized organizations have long outlived their usefulness. The behemoth plods on - and the "new Jewish culture" is barely a grass-blade underfoot.

No matter how many philanthropists are starting to "get it," there simply is not enough money going into small, innovative Jewish upstarts - yet. (It would have been nice to be paid for writing this article, for example.) Were the measure cultural rather than conjugal, there is no question that the groups that do exist are having an impact. So Called, for example, has collaborated with Wu Tang Clan's Killa Priest, and Matisyahu is currently on tour with Trey Anastasio, from the iconic jam band, Phish. One cannot help but wonder how much more of an impact "new Jewish" cultural and spiritual organizations could have if their share of the Jewish funding pot increased from .01% to .02.

Fortunately for his fans, So Called would probably minimize these questions, preferring instead to focus on a dope new beat, or the sweetness of an old forgotten melody. He is fortunate, leaving it to Bisman and others like him to cultivate relationships with visionary philanthropic individuals and organizations. There is an implication in much of the Jewish community that Judaism is a product that needs to be marketed and sold. But for So Called, it's something to be sampled, transformed, and changed into something new. Maybe the conservative side will prevail, and only those organizations which repeat the same shopworn "truths" will gain mainstream support. Or maybe, over time - as these innovative startups grow into established Jewish organizations - the "Jewish experiences" they create might change the face of mainstream Judaism itself, into something more inclusive, more compelling and - if So Called has anything to do with it - more funky as well.

Orly Cogan, *Shiva*

Masoretic Orgasm

HAYYIM OBADYAH

You know the number of freckles on your lover's nose.
 Shall I not count the verses beginning with וְאֵלֶּה?
You trace the line of a cheekbone,
 And shouldn't I take delight in pairs of words with and without
 הֵא הַיְדִיעָה ?
You even love the wrinkles of experience.
 So wouldn't I relish the times that the text says לוֹ with a וָו
 but we pronounce it לֹא with an אָלֶף even though they sound the
 same?
Every מַקֵּף kisses my lips.
Each רְבִיעַ peppers the taste of the Divine on my tongue.

The Use of Mysticism

JAY MICHAELSON

What can we learn from mystical experience?

Mystical testimonies are strange texts, since they report a direct experience of something that lots of people don't believe exists. It would be one thing if they merely reported curious sensory occurrences, but most mystical texts say more: they report an experience of something - often of Ultimate Reality, whether conceived of as "God" or Brahman or, simply, the true essence of being. Moreover, they usually report a certainty of knowing, deeper and more sure than any ordinary perception. What to make of them?

Unlike most reports, mystical experiences are not usually verifiable. Saadia Gaon, the great medieval Jewish thinker, once argued for the supremacy of Judaism over Islam because while Islam depended on the experiences of one man, the Jewish revelation was witnessed by 600,000. Of course, that argument depends on the reporting text being reliable - but it points to the central problem of mysticism, which is subjectivity. Crucially, though, the problem of subjectivity applies both to the mystic and to the critic. An avowed atheist approaches the question of "what happened here" in a fundamentally different way from an agnostic or a believer, and is likely to exclude any accounts of the experience that would contradict her fundamental beliefs. A believer, meanwhile, does the same. How can we tell whether the experiences are truthful or delusional, without simply repeating our own pre-set opinions as to the existence or non-existence of God?

And finally, a Lockean problem: given the subjectivity of mystical experience, can it ever be trusted? Our time has known religious zealots, motivated by their religious experience, who have murdered thousands. Even

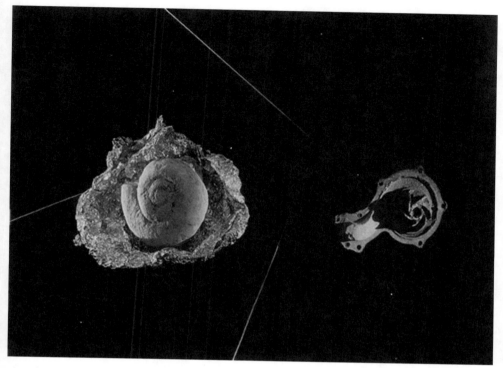

Avraham Eilat, *Still Life*

if mysticism feels good and delivers results, it may still be dangerous. So is there any use to mystical practice?

I want to look at the question of truth first, and then reflect on the question of usefulness.

In college and in grad school, I read hundreds of testimonies, tracts, and accounts of mystic quests; accounts of visionary ascents, ecstatic unions, and divine theophanies. I was entranced by the possibility that "God," that being or reality whose existence or non-existence seemed to be such a critical issue - after all, some people made it the center of their lives, while others denied its very existence - could be directly perceived, and, by extension, proven. And I wrestled with how to evaluate the reports of different mystics, since, naturally, the details of mystical experience vary from tradition to tradition: Catholic nuns have visions of Christ, Hindus of Krishna. But if these expert practitioners, contemplatives with plenty of experience with false and true intuitions, weren't just imagining things, what explains the multiplicity of experience?

The old, now somewhat musty, account provided by scholars is that ineffable core experiences (and nearly all mystics insist on their ineffability) are interpreted in religious language by the mystics. More recently, sophisticated academic readers of mystical texts have concluded that conceptual frameworks and preconceptions play a role in shaping the experience itself - that mysticism is not everywhere the same. In response, religious commentators have simply said that God manifests in different ways to different people.

Even if we can somehow either explain away or minimize the importance of differences in mystical accounts, the fundamental question remains. The subjective experience itself - the so-called "universal" experience of nearness of union, of knowledge that transcends verbal articulation - even this experience is difficult to verify. How do we know that what the mystic says happens, happens? And how do we know that it isn't all delusion?

In the last several years, I have moved beyond the reading of books like Steven Katz's "Mysticism and Philosophical Analysis" and have tried the techniques of the mystics myself. Truthfully, what impelled me to do so probably has more to do with love and yearning than with a search for empirical data. However, I have not left behind my empirical mind (sometimes to the detriment of my contemplative practice, to be honest) and so I have collected evidence myself - necessarily subjective, but, at least for myself, evidence nonetheless.

Here is what I can report. I can say, in my own, limited and subjective experience, that if you do what some mystics and contemplatives say, you can experience the results they promise. Obviously, I haven't tried every contemplative path. But I have tried more than one, and have discovered that they do deliver what is promised. It is possible to slow down the mind so much that literally watching paint dry (even if it's already dry) is fascinating, beautiful, and interesting. It is possible to scramble the mind with letter permutations and free associations so much that the thinking mind seems to let go and a strong sense of union with the All arises. And it is possible to refine awareness itself so much that the emptiness of things, and the role mental construction plays, becomes a directly apprehended reality.

Moreover, there is a sense of "presence" in these experiences that is more than a sensation of having one's mind altered. A great love arises, and an obvious certainty that the love is not just arising within the self. Rather than the self containing the feeling of love, the love seems to contain the "self" and everything else within it. When my thinking mind and desiring mind are slowed down enough, this love and compassion arise naturally, without any prodding or effort from me. (I'm very bad at prodding myself to be nicer; for me, the only way that works is to actually become more loving, sincerely.)

In other words, in highly concentrated mental states, I have had experiences that conform almost exactly to mystical testimonies and descriptions - including many I had not yet read when I had the experience. A sense of union; a feeling of peace; a sense of proximity to the Divine or the Universal. It is all exquisitely beautiful, and it can all be experienced with only a few weeks of effort.

For many contemporary mystics and "spiritual people," this is enough. It's the answer. Trustworthy, experienced writers promise a glimpse of Ultimate Reality, and an

Joyce Ellen Weinstein, *Moses and Joshua*

upwelling of authentic love - and there it is. And for many religious people, it is painfully obvious that what is happening here is an encounter with God - it fits all the criteria, it leads to expressions of love; what more could one possibly want? Why continue to doubt?

Well, I was raised a skeptic. The process of education is, fundamentally, that of acquiring the cognitive skills of doubt, of learning to take apart assumptions more critically and carefully, and I have honed these skills for many years.

This process encourages doubt, and thus can undermine some contemplative practice. Surely, though, it is better than the alternative: naïve people (one thinks of our current president, for example) absolutely convinced that the values they were taught as a child are either unquestionably correct, or so useful for society that we should regard them as such. The power of "faith" in such contexts is remarkably destructive, as we well know, but it is perhaps more remarkable that this kind of "faith" has any credibility left at all, given how many once-certain ideas - e.g., that white people are superior, that men are superior - have been relegated to the intellectual dustheap. Somehow, the idea that uncritical fundamental "values" should guide our public lives endures, despite its appalling track record, Education, as I understand it, is the slow process of awakening from the fundamentalist delusion into a more mature, critical stance toward values and claims of authority.

Applied to subjective, mystical experience, however, the same sort of critical thinking can be destructive. Were critical thinking merely a cognitive tool, there might be no problem with it. Yet often, its appearance of rigor can actually mask unjustified assumptions, and leave us perpetually sitting on the fence. For example, at a recent Seder table, I had occasion to mention the six week retreat I sat last fall. Before I even finished my first sentence, someone interrupted and said, sharply, "You're deluding yourself." "Okay," I said, proceeding to explain that, as I understood it, meditation practice was about seeing clearly - the exact opposite of delusion. It would be quite a failure, I suggested, if a 2000-year-old process meant to refine thought and concentration actually further obfuscated it. "I don't know," he replied, "but you're deluding yourself." I tried again. "Really? For six weeks?" "Well, you're deluding yourself for six weeks."

This short exchange illustrates that what is often really going on, underneath the patina of healthy skepticism, is just fear and doubt - not justified, not useful, just a certain stubbornness, grasping to some beliefs or desires about the world and not admitting that any alternative is possible. There was no dialogue at the Seder table, just a blanket refusal to admit that any meditation practice could yield anything other than delusion. Blind skepticism is as unappealing as blind faith, and just as dangerous. After all, the same person at the Seder had etched-in-stone conservative political views, and met questions about those views with exactly the same rejection. It's the attitude, not the substance, that is where the danger lies.

At the same time, certain kinds of doubt are necessary to get the contemplative process underway in the first place: doubt that chasing riches in the rat-race will really bring you lasting happiness, for example. And along the way, doubt remains a crucial ally, making sure the conceptual mind, or simple desire, isn't filling in the gaps of experience in a way that suits our preferences. For example, there are many, many spiritual seekers who use their own mystical experience as a foundation for all kinds of belief systems. A sense of intimacy, or love, leads to vast conclusions about the nature of reality ("We're all One," for example). But just because you've had an experience that feels really true to you doesn't mean it actually is true - and while it's easy to dismiss the New Age seeker as harmless, the unjustified leap she is making is not so different from fundamentalists. Once again, different substance, but same process.

So, a certain kind of inquiring curiosity - not quite skepticism, but not taking anything on faith either - is actually necessary for mysticism to work. As I'll develop below, this is one of the primary uses of mysticism as a form of social action. If you take something on faith, whether it's the belief that all this stuff is delusion, or the belief that all this stuff is prophecy from the angel Metatron, you're closed off to the potential of transformation itself. It just doesn't work. This is why the Buddha said not to believe anything he said, and why you're meant to kill him if you meet him on the road. Real mysticism does not fulfill expectations; it effaces them.

Thus, in posing the questions of what we can know about mystical experience, I think I'm not just reflecting my Jewish-skeptic upbringing. It is critical to also question the questioner, proceeding carefully between blind skepticism and blind faith. With this in mind, I ask again: how do we know that mystical experience is real? And if we can't know, what do we do with it?

The first step is remembering what we do know. I know that what the mystics promise, happens. I have experienced what they have described, by proceeding along their recommended practices. Thus, if my experience is wrong, it's not just that I'm deluded - it's that all mystics are deluded. This is a critical distinction, because there are thousands upon thousands of mystics who, across history, have devoted their entire lives to contemplative practice, with plenty of doubt and self-examination along the way. Thus, if I am in delusion, so are thousands of other contemplatives across history.

Second, and relatedly, this testimony is "expert" testimony. Contemplatives are precisely those people who have devoted the most attention to the mind and the spirit. I wonder what would have happened if, at the Seder table, I had doubted the foundations of modern dentistry to my conversation partner, who was a dentist for thirty years. "Nope, you're deluding yourself," I might have said. "Flossing does not prevent gum disease." He would presumably point to studies, but I could point to counter-studies - yet at a certain point, surely his data should "win," because it was compiled by experts in the field. Likewise, the reports of monks and nuns and mystics, are "expert" testimony. Who are you inclined to believe more - the doubter who has never once explored these pathways, or the expert who has spent her life doing so?

Third, and more subjectively, there is a sense of certainty during the experience of mystical union that is, in my experience at least, almost unparalleled. It doesn't just seem true; it feels truer than anything I've ever felt before. It is neither an inference nor a vague sense of the sublime; it is more certain than knowing your name, or knowing that you're seeing these words. It feels like "Yes, this is it. This is the core truth. This is what you have been looking for your whole life." Sometimes it carries a sense of amazement; sometimes it doesn't. At times, it feels calm; other times, it's actually very funny. But the degree of certainty it carries is beyond description.

Now, the sense of certainty is not enough. Everyone's been certain of something that turned out to be wrong - e.g., he loves me, he loves me not. Religious people in particular hate to hear this, because their "rock of faith" is the foundation of their whole lives, and they deeply don't want to question it. But as one politician said last fall, you can be both certain and wrong.

In the case of mystical experience, though, it's worth refining the inquiry a bit more, and asking what we are really certain about, and what is constructed around it. This is what I am certain of my mystical experiences: there is a real love that arises. There is only "this moment." There is no separate self. There is the knowing that that which is called the world is really arising only in Awareness - not my awareness, or yours, but your real awareness; that of the real you, which is Who you really are.

There are already a lot of concepts in there, of course - but note that the "God" concept is not, yet, one of them. This is a critical point. Suppose we were to say, for the moment, that the directly-perceived effects are all there is, without drawing any conclusions as to their source. In fact, if done without indulging in too much doubt, doing so has several benefits.

At the outset, this view of mysticism is really no different from that of the doubter, atheist, or

Saul Robbins, *42nd Street*

neurotheologian. None of those people doubt that there is an experience occurring in the mind - some just maintain that it is only in the mind. Rather than argue with these people, what if we surrendered, and agreed that there is only the experience. That which is experienced is beyond our verification. Note that we're not espousing the materialist reductionism of some critics - namely, that there is only the brain and its chemicals, and that that is really all there is. But in postponing the question of what the experience is of, we do get closer to communication.

Second, and this time from the practitioner's point of view, one can see even the most wonderful, rapturous mystical states as just a mind-state. Granted, it is a very pleasant mind-state, but, like all very pleasant things, it can turn sour with too much attachment - and it passes, and it's devoid of separate reality, just like everything else. If we are operating within a theistic worldview, the Infinite is really Infinite; although naturally more delightful, a mind-state of union with God ought not create the false belief that God is not here, in this moment, as well. So, even if the mind-state is one of *devekut*, of cleaving to God, it will pass, and too much yearning for one kind of encounter with God can cause one to devalue all the others. Of course, if we are operating within a non-theistic worldview, not reifying the experience, or inferring stories about it, is a crucial step toward discerning the truth. In either case, simply letting the experience be - without any attempt to prove anything - allows a relaxation into the experience that allows it to be appreciated for what it is, rather than for what the ego may want it to be.

Thus the attitude of "the effects are all there is" leads one to more carefully notice those effects, rather than jump into a story about what is happening vis-a-vis the Divine. This leads to a second benefit, which is a revaluing of the experience itself. This mind-state (*devekut, samadhi, unio mystica*) isn't significant because of a story about what it

represents; it's significant because it engenders more
compassion and more wisdom. Conversely, a mind-state
which may have felt very "mystical" but which brings about
cruelty or unskillful behavior is easily judged by its fruits,
rather than by the supposedly mystical feeling that
accompanied it. And one finds in almost every
contemplative tradition, theistic and non-theistic, precisely
this metric for evaluating truth. The stories cannot be
verified; but the effects can.

Third, because there is no attribution of "God" to the
mystical experience, certain forms of doubt - i.e., the doubts
throughout this entire essay as to whether the experience is
"real" - simply do not arise. Of course the experience is
real; it is happening. Without a God-concept, what else
does there need to be? One problem with the God concept
is that it simultaneously carries no attributes and a lot of
attributes. I provide an account of a sense of union, and it
is read as a union with God. But it doesn't stop there: it's a
God who is presumably omnipotent, omnipresent, and so
on. Yet are these attributes present in the experience?
What do I really know about the experience of union? I
don't know that it's with an omnipotent Being who gave his
only begotten son to redeem the sins of mankind, or
liberated the Israelites from Egypt. My heart feels it, and,
again, it matches what mystics of multiple religious
traditions say about their relationship with the Divine
Beloved. But really, those are ascriptions onto the
experience, projections, connections. Myth resonates - but
it also can insinuate itself into an experience which, on its
own, is bare of such story. And since mystical experience is
very powerful, with a strong sense of certainty, and strong
attachment, it can itself be dangerous. When mystical
attachment gets married to a myth (as discussed in greater
length in my essay from last year, "Passion and Violence"),
dangerous results can occur. Passion plus myth equals
extremism.

But it's not just Lockean prudence that keeps me from ascribing too much to my mystical experience. That would, I think, be rather dry. Don't we want to dance with God? To sing poems and chant hymns? This isn't just some Buddhist "mind-state" - this is God! So, no, it isn't just being politically correct; rather, I think that if we keep our mystical experience free from theological associations, we can come to love God even more.

Why? Because - and here is the hook - mystical theology, hewing closely to experience, actually turns out to be more careful theology. If we strip "God" of associations and concepts, we are being more faithful not only to our experience, and not only to our ethics, but to God as well. Any concept we have of God is not God; it is a finite concept, tied to the finite mind, conceptualized in terms of finite substances and ideas which, in their limitation, are not God-in-godself (a concept which itself is inaccurate, because it is a concept). If you have an idea of God, God negates your idea.

Thus, any idea or concept imposed upon the ineffable mystical experience actually takes us further from the Divine. Not because of what neurotheologians say; because of what actual theologians say. Perhaps this is why mystics are notoriously reticent about describing their experiences, even in reliable religious-mythic terms: because every term is a diminution. Think of something you'd like to say about a mystical experience - that it was truly of God, for example - and you'll see that it is actually about a concept. It is wrongly finitizing the Infinite.

From the theological point of view, an experience of Ultimate Reality is just an experience - only known to be what it actually is, namely, an experience of Ultimate Reality. From the practioner's point of view, *samadhi, devekut*, other mindstates - these are mindstates. They do exist, as mindstates. The only time we get into the whole question of "Is this real? Am I deluded?" is when we are

Gustavo Castilla

claiming an experience of something outside the self. And that is error. From a negative-theological perspective, the claim is always going to be false, because it is a claim about something. And from a nondual perspective, the claim is false because it is a claim of something outside the self. Either way, the less said, the better.

Delusion, in a nondual perspective, has nothing to do with God. It only has to do with mistaken utterances about the world of appearance.

Mysticism does give experiential access to the nondual truth, but that truth could be deduced from logic anyway, as

Spinoza did and Vedantists did, and many Kabbalists did as well. In this light, rather than see contemplative practice as proving something to be true, we might see it as *showing* something to be true - something that can be proven apart from experience, but whose power is not really felt until it is experienced. For example, it is possible to see, directly, that even one's longest-held, deepest-felt desires - the parts of ourselves we really want to call our "self" - are actually merely arisings. They appear, they disappear, and while we may conventionally refer to their agglomeration as the "self," there's nothing really there that constitutes this "self." And once that illusion is seen - not argued or proven, but directly seen - to be illusory, there is no separate self left to be uniting or not uniting with the One. There is only the One.

And the anxieties about what mystical experience does or doesn't prove subside. There is the knowing of all of these experiences, is there not? So who is doing the knowing, if there is no separate self?

Get this: if there isn't someone doing all that knowing, if there's just the epiphenomenon of knowing itself - well, that's exactly right. Because we've moved away from a concept of "someone" and toward the ineffable. After all, God doesn't have a self either. We tend to say "Being" as if a gerund were really a noun, but in that statement is a mistaken ascription of self-ness. This contradicts both Buddhist and Jewish dogma (everything is empty) and the idea of the Infinite (Ein Sof) itself. There is nothing more than all of these composites of experience. There is not a "Knower" if by "Knower" we mean some separate thing out there. God is not something in addition to the universe (if God is, then that part is by definition completely unsayable, unknowable and unthinkable). But there is a "Knower" in a more refined sense, a sense free of concepts and anthropomorphism.

There's this persistent thought that there is some

tangible God-consciousness that stands apart from all the strands of reality, and that either does or doesn't exist. But that is bad theology. It is yet again to make an error of selfhood, this time on a huge theological scale. God, also, is Empty - indeed, God is the Emptiness itself.

This is what mysticism shows. It proves nothing, but it provides a direct experience of the Knowing that is without a conventional Knower. It is more sure than dogma or syllogism, and it leads to abundant love.

If we suppose that mysticism can prove the mythic assertions of the Bible, we are mistaken. Myth is its own language, not a poor form of theology. To ask a mystic to prove that Jesus walked on water is like asking a mystic to prove a beautiful piece of music, or the significance of Shakespeare. It's a misuse both of mysticism and of myth. Consequently, when we ask "Does mysticism really prove there's a God," we are misusing mythical language, and it shows. At this extreme, the language collapses, and seems to be full of mistaken assumptions about what God is or isn't. In fact, these assumptions were never really there to begin with; they get read in by our misappropriation of mythic terms, and our misuse of myth to do something it isn't trying to do. Reading the Bible for theology is like trying to get a recipe for wine by reading a poem about drinking it.

The use of mysticism cannot lie in the realm of proof, because proof is proof-of-something and what mystics are describing is not something, but everything and nothing. Instead, the use of mysticism lies chiefly in the beauty and richness of the experience itself, which enlivens religion - I once called meditation the "answer key" to my Jewish religious practice - and unveils the reasons for poetry.

A second use of mysticism lies precisely in the undoing of mysticism as a sort of theological proof. Religion, to quote the Sufis, is a tool - a finger pointing at the moon. If you do it right, you'll behold that which cannot be described. If you do it wrong, you'll get very attached to the finger. The finger gives you good feelings, it unites you with your community, it is, according to your sacred texts, the most holy thing there is. Whether it's a strip of land in the Middle East, a society ordered in a particular way, or a truth about a piece of text, the "trigger" for religious sentiment can itself be fetishized. This is what idolatry is about: not so much the use of idols as the mistaken belief that the idols are the source of the power.

Mysticism belies these kinds of religious claims. Clearly, though there may be phenomenological differences in the experience, you can "get there" through any number of ways - even ways that a particular sacred text wants to ban or suppress. And when you do "get there," you find yourself unable to prove anything at all.

A naïve mystic prays in a synagogue, has a mystical experience, and then ascribes the experience to the particular prayers he uttered. He turns the tools of spiritual practice into magic tricks.

A sophisticated mystic enters and prays in the same synagogue, and perhaps has the same experience. But she does not ascribe the experience (moon) to a particular trigger (finger). She treasures the trigger, since it has pointed beyond itself. But there is no illusion that if the finger were lost, so the moon would be.

The fundamentalists in Saudi Arabia, the settlers formerly in Gaza, the Christian Right - all these groups do experience intense realities of life by means of their religious practice. It's not that they are deluded. They taste the energies of Divinity, and visit states of mind where many fear to tread. Their error appears when they become convinced that their myths are facts (as if Genesis were meant to be a science book), and believe that only their pathway could possibly have led to this wonderful experience. So mysticism becomes misused, and with all the more grievous results because the intense passion of mysticism gets married to the myth of religion (as described in my review of Mel Gibson's "Passion" and the violence of religious fundamentalism in a previous issue of this journal).

But if it is pursued openly, with interchange with others, and with a practice which constantly, gently questions the leaps of assumption which are all too easy to make - then mysticism undermines fundamentalism. Interpretations are seen for what they are; so are theologies and so are myths. Love encompasses it all.

Mystical experience is as the mystics say. That much I can relate to you. And the more carefully we think our theology, the less else it could or should evince. Just one last illustration: A Buddhist might report, after a mystical experience: "I feel love." A Jew might report "I love you, God." The more we can erode the difference between those statements, the closer we are to heaven.

K'ga Vna:
Just as They...

RABBI ZALMAN SCHACHTER-SHALOMI

It is said that on Shabbat we are endowed with an extra
soul or have access to a higher realm of soul. This prayer is
taken from the Zohar and expresses with great beauty the
relationship between this soul and the Holy Shabbat.

Just as they
Hesed, G'vurah, and Tiferet,
Netzah, Hod,
And Y'sod on high
become One mind and One purpose
so does She,
Malkhut here below
unite in the mystery of Oneness
to be at One with those above
to receive the Holy One, blessed be He.
The Holy One, blessed be He,
does not seat Himself
On His glorious throne,
Until She, the Sh'khina
turns to the mystery of Oneness
as He does
in order that One and One
would become One.
This is the mystery
of "The Yah is One
and God's Name is One."
The mystery of the Sabbath
Is the Sabbath Herself

It is Her uniting
with the secret of Oneness,
of uniqueness,
that She may immerse
in the Secret of One.
The prayer of the ascent of the Sabbath is the holding on
to the glorious holy throne
in the secret of Oneness.
As She, the Sabbath,
enters into union,
She sheds the side of otherness
and all judgment and harshness
pass from Her
and She remains in union
with the holy radiance
and crowns Herself
with many crowns
as She faces the Holy King.
All holders of wrathful power,
all relentless condemners
are totally confused and pass from Her
and in the whole universe
there are no sovereign others
beside Her.
Her face shines with a sublime radiance,
as She is crowned below
by the holy people
who themselves all become
enwrapped and crowned
with new supernal souls
in order that the service of worship
be a blissful one;
to praise Her in Joy
with radiant faces;
to say "*We Bless You.*"

Bara Sapir

The Fundamentalist in the Mirror
The Provincial Culture of the London Bombers

DAN FRIEDMAN

Over the past fifteen years, when explaining my hometown of Leeds to friends in Japan, America, Israel, and Europe, I have had to resort to a variety of cultural references. "Have you heard of Henry Moore, the sculptor? He's from Leeds." "Perhaps Soft Cell - you know, 'Tainted Love' - they come from Leeds," or "Remember The Who album Live at Leeds?" But as of July 2005, I no longer triangulate my hometown by means of semi-obscure art or music references, or to my beloved football team Leeds United who have seen (and will see) better days. From July 7th Leeds has gained a degree of global infamy as the hometown of the London suicide bombers.

The United Kingdom of Great Britain and Northern Ireland, usually known as the UK (Americans tend to use the word British far more than subjects of the Queen), has comprised the north western corner of Ireland (since the rest of Eire won independence 1921) and the whole of the neighbouring larger island. This larger island is split into three countries: Scotland at the top, Wales reaching out to Ireland in the west, and England taking up most of the good arable and building land in the centre, south, and east. Leeds is slap-bang in the middle of the big island, at such a strategic juncture that Hitler intended to make it the capital of Nazi Britain.

Despite the best efforts of Monsieur Napoleon and Herr Hitler, these islands and the smaller ones within easy coastal reach have been largely insulated from external attack since the Norman invasion in 1066. This made it a particular shock when three tubes and a bus were bombed by Muslim fundamentalists on July 7th of this year. There have been domestic disagreements - extremely violent ones - over the past four hundred years, but not since the days of the Blitzkrieg has truly (i.e. not Irish) foreign policy come back to roost in the British isles.

I'm shocked but not surprised that the July bombings happened. The explosions of July 7, and to a lesser extent the detonations two weeks later, were tragic and abhorrent. All reasonable people condemn them. But, although the exact details were unpredictable and original, all of the constituent factors had already been rehearsed and should have been unsurprising: a terrorist attack on the British mainland (thirty five years of the IRA), a bombing of London (the Blitz), the focus on a 'soft' transport target (Madrid, 9/11), the use of European-born suicide bombers (Richard Reid the shoe bomber), all part of violent Muslim-fundamentalist attacks on 'Western' values. 9/11 was such an iconic and massive attack that it was treated as an exception to, or a disruption of, the general state of affairs in the world. In contrast, the lack of newness of 7/7, as well as the generally phlegmatic tone of the British press and public (in all things apart from celebrity gossip), mean we can treat the event as manifestation, however extreme, of the current state the world in which we are living.

1. The Composition and Explosion of a Stereotype

Despite the cosmopolitan appearance of London, and although there have been representatives of different ethnic, national, and religious groups in England since the Norman invasion in 1066, the U.K. still has a far more homogenous population than the U.S. Small Jewish, French, and Irish populations, among others, have left local reminders of their presence but even now the combined 'minorities' (i.e. non-whites, non-Christians, non-native English speakers) account for under ten per cent of the English population.

The suicide bombers (and the attempted bombers of July 21st) were all Muslim. This, along with the IRA's recent disavowal of violence, makes it tempting to stereotype and suspect all Muslims, and only Muslims, of terrorist actions. Moreover, for most people in England the religious affiliation is linked to a racial component as well: suspecting all Muslims means suspecting all 'Asians.' When it was first suggested that the bombers were from Leeds, the immediate presumption was that they were part of the large 'Asian' community of Bradford. This presumption holds a grain of truth but that stereotypical grain can obscure the larger picture and its potential significance.

In a linguistic practice that is revealing of the Western dismissiveness of the East, the term 'Asian' is used unhelpfully and differently in the United Kingdom and the United States. In the latter it refers to someone whose ethnicity can be traced to the approximately one and a half billion East Asians who come from Korea, Japan, China, and surrounding areas. In the former, however, it refers to the nearly two billion South Asians, specifically those whose parents or grandparents came from the wider Indian subcontinent: India, Bangladesh, or Pakistan. In Great Britain (there is a negligible Asian population of Northern Ireland), according to this definition, the triangle of Asian settlement stretches from London north to Leeds and west to Manchester, including most notably Birmingham and Leicester. There are approximately two million Asians in Britain, according to the 2001 Census of Britain, and they are concentrated in urban centres: Scottish and Welsh Asian populations are, like the populations in rural England, extremely small (well below 1%).

The majority of so-called 'immigrants' from the Commonwealth - the agglomeration of nations formerly incorporated in the British Empire - came to Britain after World War II, when manpower was in short supply and

subjects of the Queen were actively recruited to come over.
As with the American slave trade, or Israel's recent
importation of Thai workers, there was little thought given
to longer-term cultural and social ramifications. In Britain,
though, the situation is somewhat different from these
other context. As the term "Queen's subjects" suggests,
there was and is a sense of connection, albeit a troubled one,
between the Commonwealth countries. Today, the
connection is seen nowhere more clearly than in sport: the
Commonwealth includes all the major cricket-playing
countries that regularly play one another in international
games, and for many, cricketing allegiance is tantamount to
national identification. Norman Tebbit - then a senior
member of the ruling Conservative Party - suggested that
if a person supported Pakistan in the Test then that was
probably his main national allegiance, effectively suggesting
that those in Bradford who regularly came to Headingley
(the cricket ground in Leeds) to support Pakistan against
England were not properly English.

The Muslim population of England is just over a
million and a half, and is concentrated in the urban centres
of the Asian triangle. Religion and race almost completely
overlap. Despite the presence, almost exclusively in
London, of a number of local converts, Muslims from
Africa, the Middle-East, and the Arabian peninsula, the
majority of English Muslims indeed do get their Islam
through the Indian subcontinental tradition. This
differentiates British Islam from the United States, where
there is a significant black Muslim population, and Europe,
where there is a Turkish and Central Asian Muslim
population. The overlap of ethnicity and religion - brought
to public attention in the 1980s by the Rushdie fatwa, issued
abroad but enthusiastically echoed by the Bradford
community - has led to the popular identification of Asian
and Muslim communities. In the last three weeks of July
this was exacerbated through the fear of further terrorist
attacks, as every backpack and every non-white face was

looked at askance. Indeed, in the weeks after the July 7th bombings, polls indicated that approximately half of the Muslims in England had thought, since the bombings, of leaving the country permanently because they feared a general backlash against Muslims.

In reality, though, neither the Muslim nor Asian populations are homogenous, nor is the overlap simple. There are several different religious practices represented in the British Asian population: Hinduism, Sikhism, Islam, Jainism, and Christianity. There are likewise many different sects, shades, and ethnicities of Muslims from around the world, the vast majority of whom are opposed to violence. Although it is a laboured point, it is important to point out that, while it is sensible for professionals to responsibly narrow down the field of suspects, we should beware of widespread systemic and social stereotyping. After all, Yigal Amir didn't make kippa-wearing Jews a suspicious community in Israel (though more recent Jewish terrorist attacks have caused many to regard young "settler" types with a suspicious eye), Timothy McVeigh didn't make people suspicious of white folk in Oklahoma, and Dr. Harold Shipman (who killed tens if not hundreds of his patients) didn't make doctors outcasts in Manchester. It is part of the terrorists' aim to shape a nameless fear and project it onto an innocent minority, in that way goading the "Western" world to engage in precisely the clash of civilizations that is already perceived by many conservatives. Generalizing rage is perhaps understandable, but it plays directly into the strategy of the terrorists.

2. Bend it Like Prasad

People whose knowledge of Britain's multicultural society come from the smash film *Bend it Like Beckham* might wonder how, or why, there would be any suicide bombers coming from England. It is true that there has indeed been a huge, benign interest in Asian culture in

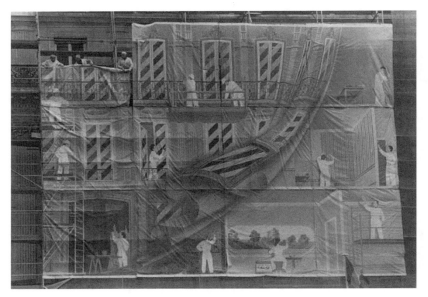

Avraham Eilat, *Urban Landscape*

Britain that has grown over the past 10 years or so. On the
music front, Apache Indian was a huge success (ironically
exporting well to India), Cornershop were a crossover pop
success bringing in traditional Indian music to simple pop
songs, Bhangra swept up drum and bass to be the last big
dance wave, and Talvin Singh, Nitin Sawhney, and Asian
Dub Foundation have won critical acclaim. In a further
move against blandness, curry has overtaken fish and chips
as the most widely eaten dish in the country (rather like
Salsa replacing Ketchup as the condiment of choice in the
U.S. in the early 1990s). As well as the ubiquitous "Curry
House" there are a number of new upscale "Indian"
restaurants (often owned by Pakistanis or Bangladeshis)
serving gourmet fusion and traditional foods to appreciative
punters of all colours and creeds.

Those on the Left who view this interaction with
distrust claim that the delight has come at the cost of

assimilation. Although mainstream clubs now rock to Bhangra melodies and rhythms, the rap that the MCs perform over the top of the music comes straight from Hip-Hop. And, after all, these are Western clubs: this is an exciting fusion of cultures, but only in a particular place, in a particular way. At the very least, this acculturation brings into question the price of enthusiastic cultural acceptance, or as a lesser goal, a tolerant multiracial society. Indeed, even the title of *Bend it Like Beckham* points out that Jesminder's guiding aspiration is to "bend" and emulate a white man - a professional footballer. It so happens that the aspirations in the film are those of a young Sikh woman - but her skill is at a game whose globally-accepted rules were codified in Cambridge, authorized in London, and played by relatively few people in the Indian subcontinent. It can feel, especially to other second generation Britons, that the price paid for acceptance by small minorities is the need to ape the white Christian majority.

The complexities of race and British identity have featured in numerous British cultural products over the last several years. For example, in *Goodness Gracious Me*, the tendency to over-identify is satirized by two couples who outdo themselves to be more British than the other. Ironically, this desire to assimilate itself marks one as an outsider; in the 2001 census only 48% of the entire population of England said they would identify themselves as British. And in the "Back Where They Came From" TV special, two couples desperately hiding their names - Dinesh becomes Dennis, Sanjeet becomes St. John, and Kapoor becomes Cooper - end up in India by mistake (they were intending to go skiing in Switzerland) and are appalled and totally discombobulated by the country and its inhabitants. Their antics are deliberately comic, and the show laughs at a number of stereotypes of Indians, white English, white English trying to be "native" in India, and Indian-Brits being extremely non-Indian. It also plays with the generational distinction between the parents who ham up the rôle of "Britisher" and the children who have little truck with this excessive rôle-playing, primarily because they are more fully acculturated, from accent to dress to attitude to career.

Some groups welcome these amusing gaffes, enthusiasms, and tendencies on the part of the successively-acculturating generations. They find it an endearing side-effect of having a fresh perspective engaging with an existing culture. Others, however, from those being emulated to those who cannot even countenance the emulation find it obnoxious. On one side this can lead to Morrissey's "Bengali in Platforms" track, or Enoch Powell's "Rivers of Blood" speech, while on the other side the younger generations of the ethnic communities can find their parents embarrassing to the point of shame.

The effects of the naïve shame of acculturation is well depicted in Udayan Prasad's 1997 film *My Son the Fanatic*. Rather than looking at a young girl trying to make it as a footballer, the film (based on a short story by Hanif Kureishi, who, like Salman Rushdie and V.S. Naipaul, has been depicting the intersections of British identity and Asian identity for decades now) portrays the drama of Parvez (Om Puri) coming to terms with his son's rejection of Western culture and adoption of a stringent form of Islam. In the wake of 7/7, we might see these actions of Parvez's son Farid (Akbar Kurtha) as expressing his shame at a rich cultural tradition capitulating to a more powerful, but crassly materialistic culture.

Farid's understanding of both his Pakistani Muslim heritage and the English culture that surrounds him is tragically inadequate. His Islamic beliefs are idealistic and unrealistic, totally unlike the experience of Islam in Pakistan, either as explained by his father or implied by the Imam he brings over. Conversely, Farid's knowledge of English culture is heavily weighted to the lived experience of a working-class neighbourhood in an economically depressed former mill town, rather than dwelling on the principles and achievements of English culture.

This dual mistake - which is interesting to ascribe to the London bombers, although to do so is, of course, mere speculation - leads to the fetishization of the metropole that is the quintessential hallmark of the provincial rebel. In other words, faced with the poor choices of culture and opportunity provided by the provinces, the young rebel blames the capital in disgust or looks to it with wonder. In *My Son the Fanatic* Farid does both - he idolizes Islamabad and reviles London. If he had gone to Islamabad he may have ended up disappointed by his unrealistic expectations; if he had gone to London he might have been pleasantly surprised. Previously the disappointment at the lack of opportunities in the material capital - New York, London, Paris - has been the key recruiting tool for subversion over the past two centuries, now it is their supposed spiritual vacuum as portrayed by the media and internet.

Farid is emblematic of the second generation's rejection of their parents' assimilationism -- not unlike the *baal tshuva* children and grandchildren of avidly secularizing American Jews. Parvez is a taxi driver who symbolically links the world of Pakistan (from where he emigrated as a young man) to that of Bradford: not only is he a taxi driver ferrying people backwards and forwards, but the name of the taxi service is "Bridge" taxis. But Parvez' taxi light keeps breaking, a symbol of his double failure. He has managed to convey neither his love of western culture (whisky, jazz), nor his understanding of Pakistan (doctrinal bullying, beautiful countryside) to his son.

Concurrent with Farid's rejection of "western materialism," Parvez falls into an affair with Bettina / Sandra (Rachel Griffiths) - the local (white) whore with the heart of gold. Meanwhile the group that has gathered around the Imam wants to fight Western immorality and depravity, eventually physically attacking prostitutes and burning down one of the houses where they gather. *My Son the Fanatic* has many faults but it does pull together many of the strands of contemporary British life that have led to the disaffection of Islamist and Leftist youth with the increasing materialism of daily life. The actions taken to counter this trend have led to the association of Islam and terrorism in both understandable and misguided ways.

3. Materialism and fundamentalism are twin shames

The modern world, created largely under the stewardship of the West, is a complicated one and, thanks to the Internet and the global economy, one whose complexities seem omnipresent. This leads to a well-recorded yearning for simplicity -- or, as Farid puts it, "purity." Extreme ideologies are comfortingly simple in a complex world, and they do provide an avenue to transcendent (or at least alternative) experiences which the "materialistic" culture of the West seems to deny. Whether religious, nationalist, or political, an ideology with an authority and a sound-byte doctrine is more appealing than the grey indecision of political integrity. This is not to judge religion, patriotism, and political ideology, but merely to point out that their responsible practice takes time, information, and discussion. The ordinary formula of religious fundamentalism, however, engenders precisely the opposite process.

Yet to suppose that the yearning for simplicity is merely the provenance of religious fundamentalism is, itself, a symptom of that same mistaken yearning. In fact, the short-circuiting of reason that takes place in religious fundamentalism is remarkably similar to that of Western "materialism." In the same way that some people would rather choose a ready-made item endorsed by a favourite celebrity than spend time thinking about the ramifications of their decisions, fundamentalism invites a short-circuiting of introspection and doubt, and an express route to the

past which it then seeks to "recapture." In the case of *My Son the Fanatic*, Farid chooses to look back to a tradition (Islam) and a homeland (Pakistan) to which he feels a connection - but he has no lived knowledge of either, and no sense of the living complexities of the tradition or nation. It is sublimely easy to imagine a 'pure' *umma* free from vice, or a 'pure' Israel free from Arabs if, like the American Israelis of the West Bank, one grows up with no experience of the inevitable complexities and compromises of actual political life. It is no surprise that, like pop stars, suicide bombers are almost all young. The virtues of youth - energy, commitment, belief - are exactly those that, coupled with the faults of youth - impatience, inexperience, solipsism - can lead to extreme acts and measures.

4. Muslims are the new Jews

The struggles of the Middle East, and Israel in particular, are always invoked in discussions of how Islam engages politically with the world. The close identification of the Islamists with the Palestinian cause is, in general, an opportunistic one, based on a shared religion and a similar rhetoric of victimhood. The similarities are, in general, artificially shaped, rather than naturally occurring. Parallels could just as easily be drawn with the persecuted moderate Muslims of Iran, the persecuted Muslims of Saudi Arabia, the outlawed Muslims of China, but the easy image - the eye-byte - is the fraught situation in Israel / Palestine.

British Asian Muslim youth may see themselves as being like the Palestinians, but the more instructive comparison is with the American/Israeli Jewish community. In both cases, a rebellious youth culture develops in response to the assimilationist tendencies of the elder generation. Both youth cultures embrace religious fundamentalism as part of their rebellion against the Western culture which their parents (or in the American Jewish case, grandparents) sought so avidly, and find within that fundamentalist world imams and rabbis who are happy to preach the right-wing gospel. And, at least as applied to the *baal tshuva* community living in America, the West Bank and Israel, both adopt right-wing political stances as part and parcel of their ideological rebellion. On occasion, this leads to violence, as in the London bombings and the acts of settler violence that accompanied Israel's recent withdrawal from Gaza.

Consider, too, the centrality of sex in religious-political struggles that would seem to have little to do with it. The final insight that *My Son the Fanatic* has into the mind of the fanatics who fill the ranks of suicide bombers and their accomplices is the importance of sex and the emotional responses that surround it. The film starts with Farid's relationship with Madelaine, which fails, and about which he feels shame - despite the fact there seems little cause. The film ends with Parvez' relationship, about which he feels no shame, despite there seeming ample cause. This figuration of the West as lover, wife, seductress, whore, is echoed in every other film about Asians in Britain including *Brothers in Trouble, East is East, Sammy and Rosie get Laid* and also, with appropriate gender change, in *Bend it like Beckham.*

The openness of sexual mores in progressive Western culture is mistrusted by fundamentalist religionists of all stripes, Christian, Jewish, and Muslim. Mostly this is reflected in the censorious statements made by the moralizing minority (Christian in the United States, religious Jewish in Israel), but a recurring motif in the mythology of suicide bombers is how they will be greeted by *houris* in the afterlife. Instead of dealing with and negating their physical, sexual, desires, the bombers externalize and project them onto a whorish west, either in the guise of a particular person (as shown in the films) or in the general rhetoric (as demonstrated by Al Qaeda). In the act of destroying this external figure in a suicide of self-cleansing, they purge themselves of shame and ready themselves for a pure consummation. Their purification comes through a self-flagellation that is carried out on the world at a terrible cost of lives.

In this light, the London bombers are not unlike the people who attack prostitutes in *My Son the Fanatic*, the Haredi protestor who stabbed three marchers in last June's Jerusalem Pride Parade, and the Christian conservatives who scapegoat gays and other sexual minorities in America. All are petrified by the secularizing advance of Western materialism. All focus on sexuality as the site of that degradation. And a small minority responds with violence.

Of course, there are some important differences. British Asian youth face far more discrimination than do their relatively privileged American (and Israeli) Jewish counterparts. Whereas British Asian youth are rebelling against a Western culture that continues to reject them, Jewish youth are rebelling against a culture that has more or less accepted them. Jewishness is also much more easily erased than Asian ethnicity. Only a minority of Jews carry the stereotypical Jewish physiognomy; the rest of us can pass. Of course, the most significant difference is the role of violence. Many *baalei tshuva* espouse rhetorics of violence, as regards Arabs or Palestinians or Muslims, but very few actually put their rhetoric into practice. Yet one wonders if the percentage of Israeli settler youth who engage in acts of violence is really that much lower than the percentage of British Asian youth.

It may disgust some Jewish and Christian Right Wingers to ponder how their great enemy in the "clash of civilizations" is so similar to themselves. Yet the moralizing American Right, the moralizing Islamic Right, and the moralizing Israeli Far Right, are all searching for meaning in a world where a materialistic capitalism that venerates only the aggregation of wealth seems culturally ascendant. For the Islamists and the Israeli settlers, this opposition is clear and explicit: both groups would be happy if Tel Aviv simply ceased to exist. For the American Right, it is more complex. On the one hand, the American Right's rhetoric is all about the "free market" and liberty. But on the other hand, the American *moral* Right is horrified at the sensual and sexual excesses that come with liberty, and is scrambling to counteract them.

Moreover, all three groups replicate the over-simplifying logic of capitalism in their rhetoric of opposition to it. Reducing both their imagined opponents and their Edenic ideals to caricatures, they enact a postmodern pop culture version of religious crusade: a rebellion of surface. The political logic of capitalism creates its own McEnemies. As the population under the sphere of influence of Western capitalism increases, more and more people are increasingly alienated, and brought into superficial contact with a crass global culture of desire. Thus the likelihood of a violent opposition increases. The London bombings are a result of this tiny percentage ready to engage in violence, just like the massacre of twelve Arabs by a machine-gun-toting Jewish man on an Israeli bus.

5. One World is Enough

Given the perverse nature of fundamentalism - it fights against Western capitalism in the mode of capitalism itself - it can thus be better understood why the violence of religious anti-capitalists is so often directed at innocent bystanders. The London bombers and others like them act from an unrest born, in large part, from a desire to reconcile worlds such as Pakistan of a generation ago with worlds such as contemporary Bradford. The perceived link, incorrect but not without merit, is that a de facto global hegemony of Western capitalism has consolidated power over the past generation, and is thwarting the advancement of the 'Third World' in the same way it thwarts advancement of disempowered minorities at home. With the fall of the Soviet Empire, the G8, the UN Security Council, and the WTO now rule whatever of the world is not dominated by the United States. Such a hegemony is a threat to economic equality, cultural respect, and diversity of lifestyles.

It is now meaningful for masses of people to talk about themselves as living in "one world." The vast expansion of the world's money markets, the physical threat of climate change, the presence of a single global superpower, mass simultaneous global media - all these have led to an understanding that we live in a single world, and that the governing power does not seem to have the interests of all the world's citizens at heart. This is not necessarily because the U.S. is racist: state politics is always selfish. Transnational entities, meanwhile, are either part of the problem or ineffectual. In this context, Islam seems like one of the few alternatives to White Judeo-Christian Capitalistic Colonialism.

Resistance to the global hegemony is difficult. Partly because the perception of hegemony relies on a wilful misunderstanding of the differences between the various world powers, and partly because the underlying capitalistic ethos is a protean one, there is neither a specific target to attack nor a specific ideology to oppose. That is why the two main types of target are symbols of power and public transportation. The terrorists perceive themselves as resistance fighters for a way of life that is threatened by the global upper classes constituted by the populations of Western countries. Britons and Americans mourn their innocent victims - but, from the perspective of those shadow-boxing against global capitalism, there may be no non-innocent targets to hit.

These groups, in short, are actually fighting against large structural trends: globalization, secularization, and the expansion of personal liberty. Yet their acts of violence are directed against specific actual people, and the opposition that the violence engenders tends to outweigh any "benefit" the violence may actually bring about.

Nor is the bewilderment of the "Western" populace especially surprising: the ramifications of the remote wars that are fought, and the economic colonialism that is carried out in their name, is hidden from them. The occasional "Not in Our Name" protests fail to highlight a system of injustices that are indeed carried out in our name. On the other side, the British Islamists' mistaken identification with the occupied population of Iraq, or Palestine, is compounded by the misguided lack of identification with the population of London. If what is at stake is global justice and an end to the slaughter of innocents, then the place to start is not by killing innocent victims. Still, despite the Orwellian nomenclature being used in the United States, we are not at war, nor on a crusade. Nor is this a clash of civilizations. Without belittling any of the losses of life since 1989, the historical over-dramatization of the situation dignifies the extremists on either side.

Parvez ends *My Son the Fanatic* by walking around his house, alone, turning all the lights on and carrying a glass of whisky out of the basement. The future of his relationships, and of race relations in West Yorkshire, are left open to examination and open to question. Previously, religious movements have preached salvation, whereas the market only promises escape. One wonders, however, if Yehuda Amichai was correct in predicting the reverse: that salvation will come not from weighty religious/historical structures, but from the everyday joys of ordinary life. If recent history is any guide, Amichai was right: redemption is more likely to come from the spark of joy between a Pakistani taxi driver and a Western prostitute he drives home, than from the righteous hatred of a son who idolizes an Imam with feet of clay.

No Places Like...

ANAT LITWIN

The images on the following two pages are taken from an upcoming exhibition at Makor, a Jewish cultural center in New York City - entitled *Sugar Plums* - which grapples with questions of how "home" is constituted in art and in culture.

The feeling of home is subjective. Without a coherent authority imposing the meaning of home, we are free to refer to existing cultural notions of comfort and stability, and to reevaluate their validity on a more personal, intimate level. Possibly the artist's main task is to create the value of home through the work of art itself, through culture, within landscapes of soul and spirit. Together, the collective and personal nostalgia they carry of a place once called home triggers the essential question: when does one feel at home?

Lior Grady (next page) has been exploring questions of private and public space for over ten years. He once created an installation piece in his own apartment in Jerusalem, removing fixtures and walls and replacing furniture with such objects as a gigantic folded paper boat and a bathtub filled with water and black hair. For *Sugar Plums*, he responds to the exploration of "home" by bringing his own bed and other personal objects into the Makor gallery.

The Sukkah Project, a collaboration between Jeremy Nadel and Merav Ezer (following page), traces the sacred and secular features of the transitional home. Through the creative process, the artists attempt to provide a spiritual shelter that connects the mundane and the transient, inventing a structure that functions as a connecting device, a space for dialogue and inspiration.

Sugar Plums will be on view through November 4.

Above: Lior Grady, *Belongings*
Facing page, top: Merav Ezer, *Nomad Land house #2*
Facing page, bottom: Jeremy Nadel: *Eden*

Karyn Raz, *Pola Negri*

What She Loved Most

NICOLE TAYLOR

she eats pickled herring out of the jar in the middle of the night, going to the kitchen in glasses and underwear, slim shoulders made shadow by the light of the fridge. i watch her eat the food that women are supposed to crave when pregnant, and fleetingly wonder what she might get up to eat in the night if she were.

she notices that i've followed her into the kitchen. i can see she thinks that i'm marvelling in amused disgust at her capacity to eat herring in the middle of the night. i am, a bit. but mostly i'm thinking: i love you, i love your night rituals, please don't stop.

but it's me who's standing at the fridge, looking for the jar of herring and no-one is watching. standing there, i think how much i want someone to be watching, who'll wait til i'm finished, make me brush my teeth (twice) then lead me by the hand back to bed. someone who, at the end of it all, will recall that that, more than any other single thing, is what she loved most.

Hilla Lulu Lin, *Wrapped Face*

A Floating Red

MARISSA PARELES

It got impossible to go uptown for books. I would try to sneak off in the break periods, but he kept coming after me: You need distilleries-Now an accidental border; now distilling equipment-Syrups-I don't understand what you're trying to say here. And then the rest: Meet us on the hour, on the corner, 28th and 3rd. And the men it took to get there. And the noxious heat and the worst maps. Yes. I think I tried to negotiate about kicks with the city I'd swear then I'd known stem to stern. No. The screen kept sucking me in, too. I would go down the back stairs, thinking, it's alright to leave my stuff here just for an errand, a minute, twenty after, I can make it, and then halfway I'd realize, on the street, that I'd left the list of books up there, and then cowed, cunning, holding my chest close, I'd go past that corner where no one should have stood yet, and past the guys the whole group would be waiting like a queue of ducklings or schoolboys, jaws slack, feet together, with the goodhearted but stern man at the front. & we'd set off. Distilleries? There was always something else.

The walking tour was amusing, I guess. The big plaster statue with real thorns and cufflinks, and all the endocrine specialists cramped block after block in the old temples. Historical plaques. But he led quickly, talked fast, and for all I know it was bitterly cold.

Then when we got the lists I would try heroics, cut in with a bit of the desire that loves to stand in the way of desire, climbing the ladder. Do you want to lie here with me? she would ask, one hand between her belly and the bed, one thumb almost in her mouth.

It would have been an accident either way. The great bookstores fell on their knees and got bought off about ten years ago. Now these zoos, all the books used, no longer in print, lay fierce and tired all caddy-corner along Broadway, only on those two blocks. This is what they said.

And then spring was bad, jerking off into the flowerpots in big groups, thinking about where the new trucks were going without us and what they were strewing everywhere, light like leaflets that scattered but did not dissipate. I tried to rewrite the sentences, but I got nowhere; I did not even know how a distillery worked.

After a while even the innocent excursions felt illicit, standing too close in the stalls when all we did was laugh and say, I'm going to throw up. That time in the park perambulating, but each circle someone left, guilt or just, just the work ethic, there's no time for, I have to get back to, you know. So I traveled for a long time, in my head, between the hard nerve of our building, stuck in the corner in the West 20s, past the constant cars, up the old subway line to that place where they were building a new city. I moved between these places as I'd think about you long after you were gone, going in a straight line along the endless road and stopping at the places amnesia and distance had darkened, stopping earlier and earlier each time. After all these weeks I still sneaked out past the indifferent guards into the anonymous streets. I tried to go up there. The blocks were like a jellied, hot dream, like running in deep, dry sand; most days I couldn't even find the station. The gauntlet of kneeling men sent out the kind of noise that confuses you in dreams, when someone plays the radio while you sleep. My radar was bad.

She told me that the political posters turned her off, so I ripped the low ones down with my right hand. Posters with the old words: Rights.Bodies.Battles. And maybe they still used those words in this city. How would I know? I lost desire and then I lost hope. On the long days in the room I ached to go out, to be guided. No, I mislead you. I used to walk outside alone and freely, could stop to look at the signs that were left, could look at the people passing and at the snow and believe what I wanted to believe. I was able to do this.

I used to go into the old city. I never went uptown. I went down to the river, to the dock, and we got high there, so that we couldn't feel anything, and we looked at the burned and gutted valley on the other side of the ships. When I slept in the dormitory bed I dreamed of knots that were animals that were knots.

We were walking out in the quad past the moonlit vigil. The president was speaking about the invasion. We took candles from a woman on the edge, we lit them from other candles, maybe in that moment we felt like brothers and sisters, or like fire could spread, he was speaking on and on about the nation, we walked through with the wax all over our hands but that moment was lost, and we watched TV for a few minutes while watching was innocent, we watched them load and launch and then there were sundaes at dinner, all hot and cold, all melting and stiffening and disappearing and sweet, and many colors, we ran to get them and to sit at those hard wooden tables eating them with a metal spoon, at the places we'd saved with our identification cards, which we took a chance on losing, we had no sense of their worth, and you started talking about the soccer game and the holiday and how much we had to do before it, and there was that stretchy marshmallow stuff under the hot fudge, which you said was too stretchy, not soft enough, but I thought it was fine. I thought it was good. I walked across the courtyard alone and thought about your departure. And I forgot what we'd been saying and tried to strike it up again but I don't know, it didn't catch, the mood was gone, we fell back into silence.

And the city outside started to fade. I got used to the noises at night so I couldn't say when they started to go. One night in the old city we heard them again, when I saw you in the flesh, in your clouds and clouds of smoke telling me not to touch you telling me to touch you, your neck against my face burning slower than the city, we heard the noises out on the back terrace with the big clock above us and our faces sucking smoke through the plastic tube and some cat fight, and the cat scratching at the screen window, and all the car noises around us and the crickets. I wanted to stay inside by the radiator, I wanted to touch it with my wrists and hips and shoulder blades, to never leave it. I wanted to read the books on the shelves. The lovers sat on the couch together, sucking each other's thumbs. If I can just get through this winter. Do you have children now? Do they sing like you do, in your sleep? Anyway, when you come back to me I will roll them through the supermarket, asleep in their twin stroller, too old to be mine, but no one will stop me or take them away. The others went in and out of the rooms. I tried to download enough stuff to keep me warm. If I can just get through this winter. I got paid to sit at the desk downstairs, where I sent you e-mail after e-mail, angering you, I could tell, where I rocked on my heels with fat tears on my cheeks and scared away the solicitors. I looked in the videocam to see who was outside. It was the same ones coming in and out.

I read the report quickly, tearing out my eyelashes and not bothering to check facts. I wrote up a summary. I pasted the picture. These things are considered now to have happened as I described them. I have no doubts. The water was running low. Disks and jars of goo and garbage lay all across the desk. My phone was charging in a cradle by the door. I wanted to be able to grab it if I had to go. Across the hall a familiar song played again and again. Friend or enemy?

The courtyard rises red through plastic wrap, red and at an equal distance. I rise out of bed, pull the phone from under the pillow and throw it in my bag. I'm going out again. Maybe today you'll get a calling card, you know? The courtyard swells and falls, swells and moves in circuits. Was I lying to you about my vision? Today it doesn't seem

so. Everyone's out without me, but no one walks out here.
The game's at the stadium. I hate this room, how it follows
me around. I turn to you finally. Stop with the anger, it
doesn't suit you. Wait, I'm sorry. But I start to breathe too
hard, I'm afraid I'll choke you. We settle for holding hands.
I go into the classroom without turning off the phone,
because, what if today you get a calling card but you can't
afford a lot of minutes, or it's hard to find a phone, or there's
a long line and you can't call back even though you want to,
or what if you figure you'll call once and see what happens?
Or what if you're in trouble? What if you're hurt, or sick? I
am studying to become you, I fill my body with pictures that
I took in secret, it's true and not madness or bad vision that
my body is filled with a hot, floating red, and I fill that red
with you.

Winter Light Promises

JACOB STAUB

Western Snowy Plover the sign reads
as I arrive at the ocean from 44th Avenue.
White feather balls, huddling, fluffed,
sitting motionless like targeted ducks.
Do not feed them, it says.
Do not let your dog chase them.
They are endangered,
presumably because they do not move as I approach,
remaining still as the other gulls squawk and swoop around them.

The mid-morning sun hazes through the mist
as I maneuver through sand-encrusted seaweed,
looking for a shell or stone, a memento of my thanksgiving,
bewildered at blessings unexpected.
Grace startles, by definition.
I unzip my windbreaker and wipe the sweat from my eyes
as I squint at occasional joggers on the promenade above,
but I can't see clearly through the mist.
I get sand in my shoes.

You too did not flinch at my approach last night-
a stranger, knocking on your door.
I wonder if this is how the visitors felt
at the entrance to Abraham's tent.
Did he know they were angels?
You seemed to, greeting me like the messenger I might be.
Did he offer them herbal tea as he seated them on pillows?
Did he lean forward, face radiant, drinking in their every word?
Were they soothed by his presence?
They announced the birth of his son,
but did they notice their own yearning to linger
in the cushion of his presence,
wondering why they had waited so long to respond to his
invitation?

Did he gently coax them to show their wings
by undressing his own soul?
Did he light candles with them?
Was it Hanukah in Beersheva?
Did the rays of the desert sun soften the December
morning chill?

You too did not flinch when I placed my right hand on
your right hip,
brushing the ridges of your spine on the way.
Decades ago,
I would play with the pigeons in Riverside Park.
They did not flee at my approach, step by step, slowly,
mindfully,
keeping my torso still above my inching feet.
They backed up the Hudson, pigeon step by pigeon step,
for blocks at a time.
God knows, they did not scare easily.
Raccoon wannabes, they would have backed me off of their
turf if they could have.
Unlike western snowy plovers, they are not endangered.

And you,
you rested your left hand on my left shoulder
as the sun set yesterday,
as we stared at the candles.
These candles are sacred, I chanted in the nusakh of my
Hungarian zayde,
the Jacob for whom I am named.
*These candles are sacred, and we are not permitted to use
their light for any purpose-except to behold them,
to be reminded of miracles past and in our own day.*
The wonder of being touched
lightly, tenderly, unconditionally.
The promise that two might dare not to back away
and yet not be endangered.

Contributors

Andy Alpern (www.golemproductions.com) is a photographer and artist based in Moshav Amirim, Israel.

Ethan Backer says that "photography is my weapon, my tool, my instrument and my pen."

Kitra Cahana is a widely-published photographer whose photographs from Israel in 2005 have appeared on the front pages of the New York Times and USA Today.

Jose Campos is a photographer based in New York. His work has been shown on three continents.

Gustavo Castilla began creating photographs when he was ten years old and has had a passion for photography ever since. He has had images published in various magazines including Time Magazine, Hola and Figaro.

Orly Cogan (www.re-title.com/artists/orly-cogan.asp) is a New York City based artist who alters vintage printed fabrics and found embroideries into a fantastical, exotic dialogue between the old and the new. Her art deals with history, tradition, mythology, nature, and intimacy.

Julie Dermansky (www.jsdart.com) is a multi-media artist whose current work focuses on documenting genocide sites around the world. She has completed public art projects and has shows her work internationally.

David Ehrlich is the author of two short story collections in Hebrew, most recently *Blue 18*, published last year by Yediot Aharonot. He's also known as the founder and proprietor of the Jerusalem café "Tmol Shilshom."

Avraham Eilat (www.pixelpress.org/eilat) was born in Tel Aviv in 1939. He was a member of kibbutz Shamir in the Upper Galilee, the chairman of Pyramida Center for Contemporary Art, Haifa, and the chief curator for the Tel Hai Museum of Photography,

Dan Friedman, Ph.D, is associate editor of *Zeek,* and has written widely for print and television, including *Da Ali G Show.*

Rabbi Jill Hammer, Ph.D, is the co-creator of Tel Shemesh: Celebrating and Creating Earth-based traditions in Judaism (www.telshemesh.org).

Leah Koenig, assistant editor of Zeek and associate of Hazon, is the epicenter of the New Jewish Culture.

Hilla Lulu Lin (www.nogagallery.co.il) was born in Israel in 1964. Much of her work focuses on the human body, and she often uses herself as both subject and object in her video, photography, installation, poetry and performance.

Anat Litwin is the director of the Makor Artists Network.

Jay Michaelson (www.metatronics.net) is chief editor of *Zeek*, a contributor to the *Forward*, director of Nehirim: A Spiritual Initiative for GLBT Jews, a teacher of Kabbalah and contemplative practice (www.learnkabbalah.com), and the author of *God in Your Body* (forthcoming, 2006).

Rebecca Mostov is a poet and Editorial Assistant at the University of Michigan Press. She won the Summer Hopwood Poetry Award in 2004.

Hayyim Obadyah, a writer based in New York, is developing the "Sacred Splendour" series of prayer books, providing modern, gender-sensitive English translations and egalitarian options for the traditional Jewish liturgy.

Marissa Pareles's work has appeared in *Best Lesbian Erotica 2003*, *Girlfriends*, *Current*, *Common Sense*, and *Lambda Book Report*. She is a Yiddish and queer nationalist, and an editor of GO NYC magazine.

Karyn Raz (www.karynraz.com) holds a degree in Art Semiotics from Brown. In her work, she expresses observed and imagined worlds with a blend of honesty and humor.

Saul Robbins (www.saulrobbins.com) is a photographer interested in the ways in which people move through, relate to, and occupy their environments. He teaches photography in New York.

Bara Sapir's (www.barasapir.com) academic, artistic, and spiritual work is fueled by the dynamic interface between creative expression and Judaism. She is an adjunct professor at Montclair State University, a leader of creativity and spirituality workshops, and art editor of *Zeek*.

Rabbi Zalman Schachter-Shalomi is a founder of Jewish Renewal, a recent holder of the World Wisdom Chair at Naropa University, and the author of many books, most recently *Jewish with Feeling*

Rabbi Jacob J. Staub is Professor of Jewish Philosophy and Spirituality at the Reconstructionist Rabbinical College, and directs its program in Jewish Spiritual Direction. He is co-author of *Exploring Judaism: A Reconstructionist Approach*.

Nicole Taylor is a Yiddishist, writer and film lawyer originally from Scotland, living in London.

Joyce Ellen Weinstein (www.joyceellenweinstein.com) has been based in the Washington, DC, area since 1988. She is among the artists included in *Fixing the World: Jewish American Artists of the Twentieth Century*.

SUBSCRIBE to ZEEK

To receive *Zeek: A Jewish Journal of Thought and Culture* in your mailbox twice per year, just follow these simple steps.

1. Write your name and address here:

2. Write a check for $14 for one year or $25 for two years to Metatronics Inc., our publisher.

3. Clip out this box (or use some scrap paper if you don't want to tear your magazine). Then, put it and your check in a stamped envelope addressed to: Zeek Magazine
104 West 14th Street, 4th Floor
New York, NY 10011

4. Place the envelope in a convenient mailbox. We and the postal service will take care of the rest!

And don't forget: new content is on **www.zeek.net** every month.